RULES

CYNTHIA LORD

SCHOLASTIC INC.
New York Toronto London Auckland
Sydney Mexico City New Delhi Hong Kong

 This book was originally published in hardcover by Scholastic Press in 2006. • ISBN 978-0-439-44383-8 • Published by Scholastic Inc. SCHOLASTIC, AFTER WORDS, and associated logos are trademarks and/or registered trademarks of Scholastic Inc. • 45 44 43 42 41 17/0 • Printed in the U.S.A. 40 • First Scholastic paperback printing, September 2008 • The display type was set in CG Collage. The text type was set in CGCollage. Book design by Kristina Albertson

My deepest appreciation to:
Everyone at Scholastic Press, especially Marijka Kostiw, Kristina Albertson, Tracy Mack, and Leslie Budnick.

Tracey Adams, my wonderful agent.

The members of my critique groups, each of whom possess that rare combination of Charlotte the spider: a true friend and a good writer.

My retreat-mates who put me on the right track: Franny Billingsley, Toni Buzzeo, Sarah Lamstein, Dana Walrath, Mary Atkinson, Carol Peacock, and Jackie Davies.

With special thanks to Amy Butler Greenfield, Nancy Werlin, Amanda Jenkins, Denise Johns, Melissa Wyatt, Lisa Firke, Lisa Harkrader, Laura Weiss, Mary Pearson, Amy McAuley, and Kristina Cliff-Evans.

And to my parents, Earl and Elaine Lord, who gave me wings but always left the porch light on to show the way home.

To John, Julia, and Gregory

I love you more than words.

RULES FOR DAVID

Chew with your mouth closed.

Say "thank you" when someone gives you a present (even if you don't like it).

If someone says "hi," you say "hi" back.

When you want to get out of answering something, distract the questioner with another question.

Not everything worth keeping has to be useful.

If the bathroom door is closed, knock (especially if Catherine has a friend over)!

Sometimes people laugh when they like you. But sometimes they laugh to hurt you.

No toys in the fish tank.

Follow the rules.

"Come on, David." I let go of his sleeve, afraid I'll rip it. When he was little, I could pull my brother behind me if he didn't want to do something, but now David's eight and too strong to be pulled.

Opening the front door, I sigh. My first day of summer vacation is nothing like I dreamed. I had imagined today warm, with seagulls winging across a blue sky, not overcast and damp. Still, I refuse to grab my jacket from the peg inside the front door.

"Umbrella?" David asks, a far-off stare in his brown eyes.

"It's not raining. Come on. Mom said go to the car."

David doesn't move.

I get his favorite red umbrella.

"Okay, let's go." I step onto the front porch and slide the umbrella into my backpack with my sketchbook and colored pencils.

"Let's go to the video store," David says, not moving one inch.

"You're going to the clinic. But if you do a good job, Dad'll take you to the video store when he comes home."

The video store is David's favorite place, better than the circus, the fair, or even the beach. Dad always invites me to come, too, but I say, "No, thanks." David has to watch all the previews on the store TVs and walk down each row of videos, flipping boxes over to read the parental advisory and the rating — even on videos Dad would never let him rent. David'll say, loud enough for the whole store to hear, "Rated PG-thirteen for language and some violence! Crude humor!" He'll keep reaching for boxes and flipping them over, not even *seeing* the looks people give us. But the hardest part is when David kneels in the aisle to see the back of a video box a complete stranger is holding in his hand.

Dad says, "No one cares, Catherine. Don't be so sensitive," but he's wrong. People *do* care.

Beside me, David checks his watch. "I'll pick you up at five o'clock."

"Well, *maybe* five o'clock," I say. "Sometimes Dad's late."

David shrieks, "Five o'clock!"

"Shh!" I scan the yards around us to see if anyone heard, and my stomach flips. A moving van is parked in front of the house next door, back wide open, half full of chairs and boxes. From inside the truck, two men appear, carrying a couch between them.

My hands tremble, trying to zip my backpack. "Come on, David. Mom said go to the car."

David stands with his sneaker toes on the top step, like it's a diving board and he's choosing whether to jump. "Five o'clock," he says.

The right answer would be "maybe," but David only wants surefire answers: "yes" and "no" and "Wednesday at two o'clock," but never "maybe" or "it depends" or worst of all, "I don't know."

Next door the movers set the couch on the driveway.

If I hurry, I can ask them before they head into the house.

"Okay," I say. "Dad will pick you up at five o'clock. That's the rule."

David leaps down the steps just as the moving men climb into the van. He might not understand some things, but David loves rules.

I know I'm setting up a problem for later because Dad's always late, but I have rules, too, and one of mine is:

Sometimes you've gotta work with what you've got.

I take David's elbow to hurry him. "Let's go past the fence and talk to those men."

A little spring mud remains under the pine trees near the fence. Only a month ago, puddles were everywhere when Mrs. Bowman called me over to say her house had been sold to a woman with a twelve-year-old daughter. "I knew you'd be pleased," she said. "I told the realtor I have a girl just that age living next door and maybe they can be friends."

A few weeks later, I had stood on my porch, waving, as Mrs. Bowman's son drove her away to her new apartment attached to his house.

It feels wrong that Mrs. Bowman's not living in the gray-shingled house next door anymore, and her porch looks empty without her rocking chairs. But I'm tingly with hopes, too. I've always wanted a friend in my neighborhood, and a next-door friend would be best of all.

Usually in summer I do lots of things by myself because my best friend, Melissa, spends the whole vacation in California with her dad. This year'll be different, though. The girl next door and I can do all my favorite summer things together: swimming at the pond, watching TV, and riding bikes. We could even send midnight messages from our windows, using flashlights and Morse code, like next-door friends do in books.

And the best part, David won't have to come since Mom won't have to drive me and pick me up.

I bite my teeth together, fighting the memory of my last sleepover at Melissa's. When Mom came to pick me up, David raced around Melissa's kitchen, opening doors, looking for their cellar, even when Mom kept telling him this was a trailer and trailers don't have cellars.

"Real friends understand," Mom had said on the ride home. But here's what I understand: Sometimes everyone gets invited except us, and it's because of David.

Walking toward the van, I study the moving men. One has a blotchy face and looks all business. The younger one wears a half smile and a dirty T-shirt and jeans.

T-shirt Man seems friendlier.

"Remember the rule," I whisper, my hand pushing David's back to hurry him. "If someone says 'hi,' you say 'hi' back."

Down the walkway, I run through conversation possibilities in my head, but that one rule should be enough. There's only one question I need to ask, then I can take David right to the car.

"Hi!" I call, reaching the corner of the fence. David flickers his fingers up and down, like he's playing a piano in the air.

T-shirt Man turns around.

"Do you know when the family's coming?" I ask. "Is it today?"

He looks to the other man in the van. "When are the Petersons coming?"

"If someone says 'hi,' you say 'hi' back!" David yells. "That's the rule!"

Both men stare past me with that familiar look. The wrinkled-forehead look that means, "What's wrong with this kid?"

I grab David's hands to stop his fingers.

"They're coming about five o'clock," the red-faced man says. "That's what she said."

"Five o'clock!" David twists under my arm.

My wrist kills from being curled backward. I grip my toes in my sneakers to hide the pain. "Thanks!" I pretend I can see my watch. "Wow, look at the time! Sorry, gotta go!"

Chasing David to the car, I hear heavy footsteps on the van's metal ramp behind me, *thunk-thunk*.

David covers his ears with his hands. "It's five o'clock. Let's go to the video store!"

My own hands squeeze to fists. Sometimes I wish someone would invent a pill so David'd wake up one morning without autism, like someone waking from a long coma, and he'd say, "Jeez, Catherine, where have I been?" And he'd be a regular brother like Melissa has — a brother who'd give back as much as he took, who I could joke with, even fight with. Someone I could yell at and he'd yell back, and we'd keep going and going until we'd both yelled ourselves out.

But there's no pill, and our quarrels fray instead of knot, always ending in him crying and me sorry for hurting him over something he can't help.

"Here's another rule." I open the car door. "If you want to get away from someone, you can check your watch and say, 'Sorry, gotta go.' It doesn't always work, but sometimes it does."

"Sorry, gotta go?" David asks, climbing into the car.

"That's right. I'll add it to your rules."

The men carry a mattress, still in plastic, up the walkway next door. Someday soon I'm going to take a plate of cookies up those steps and ring the doorbell.

And if the girl next door doesn't have a flashlight, I'll buy her one that turns on and off easily.

Mom says I have to deal with what is and not to get my hopes up, but how else can hopes go but up?

"Wear your seat belt in the car," David states. "That's the rule."

"You're right." I click the seat belt across me and open my sketchbook to the back pages. That's where I keep all the rules I'm teaching David so if my someday-he'll-wake-up-a-regular-brother wish doesn't ever come true, at least he'll know how the world works, and I won't have to keep explaining things.

Some of the rules in my collection are easy and always:

Say "excuse me" after you burp.

Don't stand in front of the TV when other people are watching it.

Flush!

But more are complicated, sometimes rules:

You can yell on a playground, but not during dinner.

A boy can take off his shirt to swim, but not his shorts.

It's fine to hug Mom, but not the clerk at the video store.

And a few are more hints than rules — but matter just as much:

Sometimes people don't answer because they didn't hear you. Other times it's because they don't *want* to hear you.

Most kids don't even consider these rules. Sometime when they were little, their mom and dad must've explained it all, but I don't remember mine doing it. It seems I've always known these things.

Not David, though. He needs to be taught everything. Everything from the fact that a peach is not a funny-looking apple to how having long hair doesn't make someone a girl.

I add to my list:

If you want to get away from someone, check your watch and say, "Sorry, gotta go!"

"It's Mom!" David yells. "Let's go to the video store!"

She's on the porch, locking our front door. I'll get in trouble if Mom finds out I let him think the wrong thing. "I'm depending on you, Catherine," she'll say. "How will he learn to be independent if everyone lets him behave and speak the wrong way?"

"You're going to occupational therapy," I tell David, "at the clinic."

He frowns. "Let's go to the *video store*."

David may not have the sorry-gotta-go rule down, but he's got this one perfect:

If you say something over and over and over, maybe they'll give in to shut you up.

"You're going to OT," I say. "Maybe —"

"Maybe" is all it takes. David twists toward me as far as his seat belt allows, his eyes flashing.

I cover David's mouth with my hand so the movers don't hear him scream.

Don't run down the clinic hallway.

When David was three and started coming to the clinic for occupational therapy, I tagged along because I was too little to stay home alone. Now I'm twelve and can stay home if I want, but I still like to come. I like talking to Mom on the ride over and back and shopping in the stores across the street, and I love the road between our house and the clinic. It follows the ocean's shoreline, and I look for snowy egrets standing stick-still in the salt marshes and osprey circling, hunting fish. At high tide, waves sparkle under the wooden bridges, and I can guess the tide before I even see the water, just by closing my eyes and breathing the air through the open car windows. Low tide smells mud-black and tangy, but high tide smells clean and salty.

The clinic is a few streets from the ocean, and in the summer sometimes Mom and I walk to the waterfront park while David has his appointment. It's the only time in the week that I get Mom completely to myself and someone else is in charge of David. Mom likes to stay in the clinic waiting room so she can hear if David has a hard time, but I like when we leave because then she doesn't look away from me every time she hears him shriek.

At the clinic there's a waiting room and a long corridor of doors to little offices for hearing tests, speech therapy, and occupational therapy. David comes on Tuesdays and Thursdays to see Stephanie, a woman with kind eyes and an office full of games, swings, a trampoline, and more balls than I've ever seen outside a school playground. I think it'd be fun to go with Stephanie and do what she calls "playing," but David thinks it's work.

I wait while Mom says hello to the other waiting-room people, but as soon as Stephanie takes David's hand, I ask, "Can we go to the park? We haven't been since last fall."

"It's going to rain." Mom sits down on the waiting room couch. "And it'll be cold by the water. You didn't even bring your jacket."

"Can we go shopping, then?" I glance out the window to the line of stores across the street. My favorite is Elliot's Antiques. From the sidewalk it seems only a door, tucked between two downtown shops, but behind the door and up a musty-smelling staircase is a sign: ELLIOT'S ANTIQUES. The whole store is like an attic, full of stuff someone's grandparents once owned but had no more use for. Things not quite good enough to keep, but not quite bad enough to throw away.

"David had a hard time last week," Mom says. "I need to make sure Stephanie can handle it. Why don't we read?"

Mom crosses her legs, like she's settled to stay. I slump on the couch beside her and check if anyone looks like they'll mind Mom reading out loud. I haven't been to the clinic since my last school vacation, but I recognize the waiting-room people because their appointments are nearly the same time as David's every week. Mrs. Frost, a tiny old lady, reads a magazine in the big chair between the front windows (she brings her even-older brother for speech therapy because he had a stroke). The receptionist with her blond, beauty-parlor hair types fast on her computer. Carol, a young mother wearing a big skirt and hoop earrings, sits in the rocking chair near the bookshelf. She leans down, handing her baby with Down syndrome chunky plastic blocks from the toy basket. In the chair next to the exit, Mrs. Morehouse, Jason's mother, checks her watch.

And there's Jason. I'm not sure how old Jason is, maybe fourteen or fifteen, but even though he's almost grown, his mother stays with him in the waiting room. Jason can't go anywhere unless someone pushes his wheelchair.

I open my backpack, and Mom cleans her glasses on the bottom edge of her shirt. When I was seven, Mom began reading the Harry Potter series to me, and even though I can read easily to myself now, we still read each new book together. I never think of the characters without hearing her voices.

I pass her the book. "Read quiet."

She turns to our chapter, and I arrange my colored pencils on the couch next to me.

Hunting out the window for something to draw, I consider the line of stores and restaurants across the street, but they look tired and "between." In a week or two, the gift shop window will have splashy beach towels and plastic sand buckets, the hotel will show off the "No" lit up with the "vacancy," and the parking lot will be full of seagulls strutting between the cars and perched on the streetlights, screeching for someone to drop a bite of sandwich or a French fry.

I wish time would hurry and there'd be sailboats tying up at the landing and tour buses passing through, and I'd already have the first hellos traded with Somebody Peterson, the girl next door.

I figure by five fifteen that first hi-trading could be over. Especially if I just happen to be outside at five o'clock when she arrives.

I sink back into the vinyl couch cushions, my sketchbook propped against my knees, listening to Mom's voice changing, character to character.

There's not much new to draw in the waiting room. The same yellowed awards cluster the walls, the same books spill off the bookshelf, and the same old toys are heaped in the toy basket. And there are only two people I haven't already drawn: Jason and his mother.

I worry that glancing will turn into staring too easy with Jason, and I hate when people stare at David. But Jason's mother fidgets — crossing her legs, picking up magazines, putting them down, smoothing her short, flipped-under, brown hair — so she'd be harder to draw.

Mom said Jason started coming to the clinic after Christmas, but the first time I saw him was February vacation. That day I didn't know where to look, so I looked at his feet on his wheelchair footrests.

Maybe by drawing Jason, I could look at him easier.

Looking closer can make something beautiful.

Sometimes I can change how I feel about something by drawing it. Drawing makes me find the curves, the shadows, the ins and outs, and the beautiful parts. I solved my hating snakes by drawing their scales, tiny and silvery, overlapping and overlapping, until all I saw was how perfect they were. Can't say I'd want a snake crawling across me, but I don't have to run screaming to Dad every time I see a garden snake now.

"Should I go on?" Mom asks. "I could stop there."

"No, keep reading."

I turn to a clean page in my sketchbook and swoop a faint pencil line, beginning the outline of Jason's head: over the top, down his temple and cheek, around the bumps of jaw and chin, and back to where my line began.

I don't know what's wrong with Jason, and it doesn't seem polite to ask. Whatever it is, though, it's something big. There's a tray on Jason's wheelchair, and on the tray is a communication book. At first

Jason's book seems like a big blue photograph album, but inside it's full of word cards, not photographs. Jason can't speak, but he turns the pages and touches the cards to tell his mother if he wants a drink, or has to use the bathroom, or is mad about something.

Today he's mad — fighting mad. Jason slides his hand across his book, jabbing at cards. His fingers curl, clawlike, as his knuckle raps one word and another.

"Yes, I *know* they had a guitar," Mrs. Morehouse says, fiddling with her earring. "But I told you, we didn't have time to stop. If I had stopped, you'd have been late for speech!"

Jason stabs his book. I hope he has a "So what?" or a "Whatever!" card.

His hands twitch, and he makes rumbling-throat sounds, near to growling.

Mom shuts our book.

Jason's jaw is a little crooked, not as perfect as I drew. But if I draw how it really is, it might look like I made a mistake.

Reddish brown waves of hair sweep over Jason's brow. A few wayward strands dangle near his eyes.

Hair's my favorite thing to draw, but I only rough it in. Otherwise, I may not have time to finish before Jason's speech therapist comes out to get him.

"What?" Jason's mother asks.

I'll draw his eyes downcast, looking at his book. That way they'll be mostly lids, and it won't matter that I don't know what color they are.

"Girl don't? What girl?"

Everything falls quiet. I glance up.

Mrs. Morehouse is staring at me. "Are you drawing my son?"

My pencil freezes, midstroke.

"Just because he can't talk," she says, "don't assume he doesn't mind!"

Everyone looks at me. My fingers move over my sketchbook, finding the corner. "I'm sorry," I whisper, turning the page. It takes all my strength, every ounce, not to cry.

"A drink?" I hear Mrs. Morehouse say. "All right. Wait here."

Mom reaches over, but I scoot down the couch, out of reach.

I pick up a lime-colored pencil and swish a tiny blade of grass on my page. One eyelash-curve of green, cutting all that white.

Footsteps pass me, but I don't look up. I tick line after line, making grass.

"Oops," Mrs. Morehouse says. "It's only a little spill."

I risk a peek. If that were David, he'd be wild to get those clothes off, but Jason sits there, a dark water spot spread on the front of his navy Red Sox shirt. Maybe he doesn't mind. Or maybe he knows there isn't another shirt. Or maybe he's used to being wet. David wouldn't care about any of those things. That shirt'd be off, faster than you could blink. And the pants, too — if any had spilled there and I didn't remind him of the pants rule quick enough:

Keep your pants on! Unless Mom, Dad, or the doctor tells you to take them off.

Mom opens our book again. "Let's see, where were we?"

"Harry was about to use his cloak."

"That's right."

As she reads, I think how useful a cloak that made me invisible would be right now. If I had one, I'd throw it over my head and run out the door and across the parking lot and the street, all the way through the waterfront park to the wharf, and board the first boat I saw going somewhere, anywhere else.

Mom reads, the receptionist types at her computer, Mrs. Frost looks at a magazine, and the baby sleeps on Carol's lap, his little fingers still clutching a pink plastic block.

"HI, JASON!"

Jason's smiling speech therapist finally comes out to get him. I'm relieved to see her, even though Mom stops reading when she comes.

"How's his day been going?" the therapist asks his mother.

"He wanted to stop at a yard sale," Mrs. Morehouse says. "So, he's upset."

"Oh?" The therapist turns to Jason. "YOU WANTED" (hands pointing, pulling) "TO STOP" (one hand karate-chopping the other) "AT A YARD SALE?" (fingers flying, eyebrows arched in a question).

Jason scowls.

His therapist pouts, her finger tapping his communication book. "Sad."

I swallow a giggle. Sad? Is she kidding? If I were Jason, I'd want cards that said: "Get out of my face!" and "Go away!" and "This stinks a big one!"

The therapist pushes Jason's wheelchair down the corridor, and Mrs. Morehouse picks up her purse. "I have a couple of errands," she tells the receptionist. "I'll be right back."

The bell above the clinic door jangles as she leaves. Through the window, I watch her cross the parking lot to her van. "What do you think Jason would do with a guitar?" I ask Mom.

"I don't know," she says. "Maybe just having one would be enough."

Watching the van's red taillights, I wonder, Enough for what? But as the van pulls away, I close my eyes and make a wish. *Please go back and buy that guitar.*

In case Mom's right.

"I didn't mean to hurt Jason's feelings. I was only sketching."

"You could tell him that," Mom says.

I cringe. "But he can't answer me."

"Maybe he'll point to the answer in his book. Or maybe he'll answer in his head." Mom returns to reading, and I draw the front of a gray-shingled house, porch steps, and a front door with a doorbell. I reach for a blue-sky pencil, but pick up midnight black instead.

I hear a faraway David-shriek, and Mom stops reading to watch the corridor. But then it's quiet, and I figure David gave in and did whatever Stephanie wanted.

My drawing takes shape under my hand: lemon for the stars, cream for the moon, pine for the trees along the fence, charcoal gray for the darkened windows, all but one.

When the clinic bell jangles again, I peek up long enough to see Jason's mother isn't holding a guitar.

"HERE WE ARE!"

The speech therapist pushes Jason's wheelchair up

beside me. "I saw you drive in," she says to his mother. "He was so upset, we stopped early."

Mom slides her elbow over in a "here's your chance, Catherine" nudge. "Hi, Jason," she says. "How are you today?"

His head stays bowed, his chin almost touching his chest.

Mom's question hangs in the air. Maybe Jason is answering in his head? Maybe he's think-saying, "I'm fine, thank you."

Or maybe, "Well, I've been better."

Or maybe, he's think-screaming, "I'm in this wheelchair, you idiot! How do you *suppose* I am?"

Whatever he's thinking, his silence stings me. I lay my sketchbook on my lap. "I'm sorry about that guitar," I tell the reddish brown waves of hair on Jason's head. "I like music, too."

His head snaps up and Jason stares hard — right into my eyes. His eyes are stunning, ice blue.

Mrs. Morehouse spins his chair toward the door, and Mom stands up to help.

"It's okay." Mrs. Morehouse holds the door open with her foot. "I can get it."

I pick up my palest-yellow pencil and add a dot to my drawing, gleaming in a window. From the dot, I sweep down a shivering beam cutting the darkness. I imagine myself sitting on my bed, hugging my knees, counting Morse code dashes and dots.

A-r-e y-o-u t-h-e-r-e?

The bell jangles again. I look up to see Mrs. Morehouse in the doorway, watching me. She crosses her arms over her stomach.

Mrs. Frost drops her magazine and even the receptionist has stopped typing, her hands held above her keyboard like a conductor waiting to cue a symphony.

"Jason insisted I come back," Mrs. Morehouse says, "and tell you he likes the picture you're drawing." She turns to leave.

I look out the window to Jason at the top of the ramp. "Wait!" Lifting my page, I pull gently so it'll tear neatly. Colored pencils fall off my lap, scattering and rolling across the floor, but I don't bother with them. "If he likes it, he can have it. Please tell him the dot in the window is a flashlight."

His mother smiles. "I'll tell him."

I'm too embarrassed to watch her give Jason my picture, so I get down on my knees and hunt for colored pencils, some of which have rolled under the heater.

"That was kind of you, sweetheart," Mom says.

I slump back on the couch. Though I move my orange pencil over a fresh page, I'm only making lines. Too-busy-to-talk lines. Leave-me-alone lines.

I bear down so hard, my pencil lead breaks.

"Sorry! Gotta go!" David runs through the waiting room, heading for the door to outside, his brown hair damp with sweat. Mom jumps up to block his way.

I flip to my rule collection and add:

If you want to get away with something, don't announce it first.

If it's too loud, cover your ears or ask the other person to be quiet.

On the ride home from the clinic, the rain comes. David holds his hands over his ears, blocking the tiny squeaks of the windshield wipers against the glass.

David hears everything extra loud, Stephanie says. Milk being poured, shopping carts clanging at the grocery store, my pet guinea pigs squealing, the school bus braking as it pulls up to the corner, and the *whoosh* of the bus door opening — all those things and a million more make David cover his ears, fast as lightning.

The last day of school should've been a happy day, but I can't think of it without seeing David at the bus stop, clutching his umbrella, his head tipped way over to his shoulder to cover one ear, his hand covering the other. Ryan Deschaine said he'd steal David's umbrella if he let go of it, and David believed him. I told him Ryan was joking, but that made it worse, because David laughed and laughed in that twisted position, and Ryan mimicked David, tipping his own head way over, laughing.

I got in trouble with the bus driver because she caught me shoving Ryan. We had to sit in the front seats so she could keep an eye on us, she said. On the ride to school, I added another rule to David's list:

Sometimes people laugh when they like you.
But sometimes they laugh to hurt you.

I hope David can learn that rule by September, when we have to go back to the bus stop.

"Maybe the family next door will be moving in when we get home." I watch a heron hunting fish in the low-water area under the bridge. His feathers are dark, slick with rain. "The movers said five, but maybe they were wrong."

"Maybe," Mom says, "but our new neighbors might have a long drive, and there's always last-minute things to do when you move."

I try to hold my hope down, but it keeps popping up again. Until Mom turns the corner to our street and I see Ryan Deschaine getting on his bike, an orange newspaper bag slung on his shoulder, his curly black hair looking frizzy from the rain.

I let loose one hope, skyward: I hope he gets soaked.

David waves out the car window. "Hi, Ryan!"

"Don't say 'hi' to him," I tell David. "He's not your friend."

"Catherine!" Mom snaps, the reflection from her glasses flashing in the rearview mirror. "Don't stop David from talking to people! Not after all the work we've done on initiating conversation."

Part of me wants to tell her about Ryan, but she'll call his mother or the bus office and make it worse for David next year. Mom doesn't understand how not everyone is on David's side.

"I ran into Ryan's mom the other day and she was

telling me all the fun things the community center is sponsoring for kids this summer," Mom says. "Wouldn't you like to sign up for something, Catherine?"

Why is it the minute kids have free time, parents want to fill it up?

"She said they're having swimming lessons, tennis, yoga," Mom continues. "They're even sponsoring a few bus trips and a summer dance. Won't that be fun?"

"I have a rule against dancing," I tell her. "No dancing unless I'm alone in my room or it's pitch-black dark."

"Don't be silly. I think it sounds wonderful."

I want to say, "Then *you* do it," but that'll get me in trouble.

If you don't want to do something, say, "Hmm. I'll think about it" and maybe the asker will forget the whole bad idea.

"Hmm. I'll think about it." I lean forward, looking between the front seats, until I see the driveway next door, a long strip of rain-black tar, empty.

I fall back against my seat.

. . .

All afternoon I try to keep too busy to check my watch every fifteen minutes, but by four o'clock I can't stand waiting in my room anymore. I take my sketchbook and head for the porch where there's a good view of the neighbor's driveway. As I open the front door, I hear Mom's voice from somewhere down the hallway: "Please stop asking me, David! Dad'll pick you up at five o'clock, and that's the *last* time I'm saying it!"

I rush outside to our porch swing, worried Mom's next words will be "Why don't you find Catherine and see what she's doing?"

I draw to the steady patter of rain on the roof and cars gushing through puddles on the road.

At quarter to five, a slow splashing makes me look up. A minivan passes through a puddle and into the driveway next door.

I pull my feet up onto the swing, watching over the top of my sketchbook. A woman gets out of the van and runs for the porch, her purse held over her short hair. From the passenger side, a girl climbs out. Tall with straight brown hair falling past her elbows, she's not fat or skinny, a perfect between. She doesn't run — just walks, like the rain doesn't bother her at all.

Sitting here thinking about what happened with Jason and seeing Ryan, I figure today might be a bad-luck day, and I should let all that bad luck run out overnight before I try something else big. Plus, I haven't baked anything yet and I want my introducing day to be perfect, not me standing on her porch, dripping wet, handing her soggy cookies.

The girl follows her mother inside without once looking over to my house.

Our front door opens. "Let's go to the video store," David says, holding his umbrella under his arm. He hops onto the swing with me, squiggling my pencil line. "Seven minutes."

"Sometimes Dad's late."

Dad always has an excuse: traffic, last-minute customers at the pharmacy who've run out of their prescriptions and can't wait until morning, a salesman stopping by with drug samples. But I think even if things went just right, Dad would still be late. It's part of him, like his brown hair or his glasses or his name tag and lab coat. I gave up expecting Dad to be on time years ago, but David thinks everything a person says is the truth.

Dad works all the extra hours he can, even on Saturdays, so Mom can afford to work part-time at home. She used to have an office downtown, but David got kicked out of day care, so now she runs her tax-preparation business from our spare bedroom. The good part of having Mom home is she's around to talk to and can take me places, but the bad part is David has to come wherever we go, and sometimes I have to babysit while she meets with clients or makes phone calls.

She says it doesn't sound professional when she has to put her hand over the phone and yell, "David! Put those pants back on!"

David checks his watch. "Six minutes and thirty-three seconds."

In exactly six minutes and thirty-three seconds,

there's going to be a scene. I know it as sure as I know the window next door is open, and David's scream will travel from my porch, across our yard, and through that open window.

A red sports car zooms by on the road, puddle-spraying our fence. "Let's count cars," I suggest. "There's one."

He glances up. It's not easy to sidetrack David, especially when it involves the video store, but he does like to count cars.

A truck rolls by.

"Two!" Raising his arm, David holds it out so he can see both the road and his watch. "And five minutes six seconds."

"Well, *maybe* five minutes."

"Three cars! And four minutes fifty-eight seconds."

I give up. We count cars: four, five, six.

And he counts minutes: three, two, one.

"Remember the rule." I flip to the back of my sketchbook and show him.

Late doesn't mean not coming.

Our new neighbor's front door opens.

"Ten! Nine!" David shouts the seconds, like an announcer at a rocket launch.

The girl steps onto her porch.

"Eight! Seven!"

I scramble to cover his mouth, but David jumps off the porch swing. A car's coming. Please let it be Dad.

"Six! Five!" David yells, and the girl next door glances our way. "Four! Three! Two! ONE!"

I peek over, but the girl isn't glancing now; she's staring right at us.

"Seven cars!" David screams as the car goes past. "'"The whole world is covered with buttons, and not one of them is mine!"'"

I jump up to stop his hands, flapping now like two fierce and angry birds.

"Is he okay?" the girl calls. "I could help you look for it."

Look for it?

"Do you need help finding his button?" she asks.

"Oh! No, thanks!" I struggle to hold David down.

The truth is, I wouldn't know where to begin explaining, especially hollering from my porch to hers.

Talking to David can be like a treasure hunt. You have to look underneath the words to figure out what he's trying to say. It helps if you know his conversation rules:

Don't use two words when one will do.

If you don't have the words you need, borrow someone else's.

If you need to borrow words, Arnold Lobel wrote some good ones.

That button line comes from a story in one of David's favorite books, Arnold Lobel's *Frog and Toad Are Friends*. In the story Toad keeps finding buttons — big ones, little ones, square ones — but none of the buttons he finds is the right button. Like none of the passing cars is Dad's.

But that would take too much explaining, and the girl is already going back inside her house.

No cookies.

No trading "hi" or "my name is."

No flashlight discussion or even a "nice to meet you." Her first-ever words to me were, "Is he okay?"

"I'll pick you up at five o'clock," David whispers. A tear gleams like a tiny pearl on David's eyelashes.

My grip on him softens. "Dad's still coming," I say. "Late doesn't mean not coming."

But those words don't help. So I reach over, wipe away his tear with the side of my thumb, and say the only words I know will calm him: "'"Frog, you are looking quite green."'"

David sniffles. "'"But I always look green," said Frog. "I am a frog."'"

I pause, pretending I don't remember what comes next, though I can do the entire book word for word, by heart.

"'"Today you look very green, even for a frog," said Toad.'" David looks at me.

I nod. "Even for a frog."

David and I sit on the swing until Dad pulls into the driveway. "Ready to go, sport?" he calls, though David is already running down the steps, headed for the car.

I watch David trying to get into the car without closing his umbrella.

"I'm sorry I'm late!" Dad waves to me. "Mrs. Jesland came in at the last minute and needed her heart pills. Want to come, Catherine?"

"No, thanks."

I check my watch. Five forty-two.

Sometimes you've gotta work with what you've got.

Wednesday morning I made cookies. But when I rang the doorbell next door, and rang it again, no one answered. Mom said there's a lot to do when you move, and I should let our new neighbors get unpacked, anyway. This morning I wanted to try again, but the minivan was already gone when I went outside.

On the drive to the clinic, I try not to let my hopes run loose, but they rush with the water under the bridges. I hope the girl next door loves swimming because we have a pond a few streets away from my house (and now, hers!). I hope she's not allergic to guinea pigs since I have two. I hope she's a little bit shy and likes to draw and read, and I hope she doesn't think it's babyish to send Morse code messages.

At the clinic Mom says it's still too cold for the park. I draw sailboats bobbing on summer waves while Mom reads aloud a scene where a spell goes wrong for Harry. I catch Mrs. Frost smiling at us, and I think she's listening, too.

The bell above the clinic door jangles and Mom looks up from the pages. "Hello, Elizabeth," she says to Jason's mother. "Hi, Jason."

Jason doesn't move his head, but his eyes turn to me. "Ahhh!"

I flinch. I know Jason can't help it, but sometimes, the sounds he makes are loud and creepy.

Jason raps his communication book.

"My son wants to thank you for the picture you gave him," Mrs. Morehouse says to me. "In fact, he asked me to hang it on his wall."

Jason's mouth drops open.

I give Jason my I-hate-when-my-mom-does-that-too eye roll.

He smiles and taps his book.

"Jason is wondering if he could have your name in his book?" Mrs. Morehouse watches his hand move card to card. "So he can talk to you. Would you mind, Catherine?"

It seems weird to think of my name in some boy's communication book, but I don't know how I could say no, so I say, "Okay."

She takes a little card and a pen from her purse. Watching her, I wonder how that'd feel, to have to wait for someone to make a word before I could use it. And to have all my words lying out in the open, complete strangers able to walk by and see everything that mattered to me, without even knowing my name.

Jason grimaces at the card.

"Well, you know I can't draw," Mrs. Morehouse says. "Do you want me to put her name without a picture?"

"I could draw it." Jeez! Where'd that come from? Just popped out of my mouth without checking with my brain first.

"That'd be great." Mrs. Morehouse pulls another blank card from her purse. "If you draw on this, it'll fit in his book."

On my way past Jason's wheelchair, I study a page of his communication book so my card'll match his others. About two inches square, each card has a simple black-and-white line drawing and the word or phrase printed along the top. His book has clear vinyl pages, like an album for trading cards, only with smaller pockets to fit the word cards.

Back at my spot on the couch, I ask Mom if I can borrow the little makeup mirror from her purse. I lay the mirror and the card on my sketchbook to give me something firm underneath while I draw.

Two inches wide, two inches high: a white block, waiting for me to appear inside. But how should I look? Like my school picture, with just-combed hair and my say-cheese smile? Or like I do at home, with ponytail hair and wearing my favorite purple T-shirt? I can't decide, so I do the easy part first and write "Catherine" at the top in tiny, neat letters.

I might not be the world's best artist, but I can draw better than the stick figures and line drawings on Jason's other cards, all perfect circles and ruler-straight lines. I choose a peach-colored pencil and study my face in the mirror. I draw the slow curve of my right cheek, sweeping down to my too-pointy chin, up my other cheek, over the top of my head, and back to where my line began.

I draw how I usually look: brown ponytail, blue-gray eyes, wearing my purple T-shirt. Not a perfect circle or ruler-straight line anywhere.

Besides, Jason probably wouldn't recognize the school-picture me, anyway.

But when Mrs. Morehouse tries to slide my card into one of the little clear pockets in Jason's book, it's the tiniest bit too big. "I'll take a sliver off the side," she says, heading for the receptionist's desk. "Let me get some scissors."

Beside me, Jason taps.

"Excuse me!" I call to Mrs. Morehouse's back. "He wants something!"

She doesn't even turn around. "Would you see what it is?"

I'm scared I won't understand Jason, but she's already chatting with the receptionist. Holding my breath, I peer down at his finger pointing to —

Thank you.

"Oh." I let go my breath. "You're welcome."

Mrs. Morehouse trims my word to fit his book, and Jason lets out a loud "Ahhh!"

He says it so loud, Mrs. Frost turns down her hearing aid.

Jason slaps, Good job.

My name stands out, colorful and detailed among the black-and-white plainness of his other cards. Sandwich. Pizza. Soda. Drink. Eat. More. Good. Nice. Bad. Sad. Happy. Mad. Van. Want. Go. I'm sorry. No. Yes. Maybe. I don't know. Make. Tell. Help. Wait. Baseball. Book. Music. Guitar. Piano. Like. Please. Thank you. Me, too. Okay. Hi. Good-bye. Boy. Girl. Man. Woman. Picture. Word. Good job. What? Who? Why? and many more, all the way to Catherine.

I long to pull his cards out and add red to the van, yellow to the happy face, and thick purple jelly between the slices of bread in the sandwich. I want to show Jason I'm sorry for not-looking at him the same embarrassed way I hate people not-looking at David.

But how? "If you ever want me to make you more words," I say, "just ask."

"Thank you," Mrs. Morehouse says, adjusting her earring. "But there's no need. These cards are part of a speech program we use, and it comes with a whole book of words. I can copy whatever he needs from there."

Jason shoots his mother a *what?* look. Yes. More. Picture.

Mrs. Morehouse sighs. "Are you sure you don't mind, Catherine?"

"I'm sure." I turn the pages of Jason's communication book, reading through his cards so I don't repeat the words or phrases he already has. Which shouldn't be hard, since all his words are boring. But to be polite, I ask his mother what words she suggests I make.

"Something *you* like would be nice. Then he could talk to you about it." She pulls a stack of blank cards from her purse. "Would seven be too many?"

"Seven's fine." Taking the cards, I'm not sure what

to do. Go back to the couch? Stay here? Jason turns a page in his communication book, and my insides twist. "Well." I glance at my watch. "Sorry, I —"

"HI, JASON!" His speech therapist smiles, striding into the waiting room. "Am I interrupting something?"

I open my mouth to say no, but she's already looking past me. "How's his day been going?"

Jason taps, Good.

"He's been a bit cranky," Mrs. Morehouse says. "I think he stayed up too late last night watching the Red Sox. It went to extra innings."

"Oh? ARE YOU" (points to Jason) "CRANKY?" (gesture plus crabby face).

Jason sighs. No.

"Good, because we're going to have fun today." The therapist turns to Mrs. Morehouse and adds, "It's time for evaluations. Why don't you come with us, and I'll show you what I have in mind."

Jason tilts his head toward me, his hand moving slyly across his book. Stupid. Speech. Woman.

I cover my mouth with my hand, so I won't laugh

out loud. Jason makes her sound like a superhero: *Speech Woman! Avenger of Adverbs! Protector of Pronouns! Champion of Chitchat!*

"'Bye," I mumble through my fingers.

Good-bye. He turns his page back to touch Catherine.

If you don't have the words you need,

borrow someone else's.

At home I line Jason's blank cards on my desk, ready to draw. But choosing words is harder than I thought.

Seven white squares, full of possibility. I look around my bedroom for ideas: from the checkered rug on my floor to the calendar of Georgia O'Keeffe flower paintings Dad bought me at the art museum he took me to last summer. That's my dream — to be an artist and have people gasp when they see my paintings, like I do on the first day of each new month. I have a tiny clothespin at the bottom of the calendar pages, so I don't cheat and peek ahead — I want each month's flower to be a surprise.

On my door is a long mirror surrounded with colored sticky-note reminders: my library books are due (Bring fine money!), August 8th is Melissa's birthday (Remember it takes seven to nine business days for mail to get to California! Plan ahead!), and even a few reminders left over from school (Find lunch card!) (Project due Tuesday!). I kept those up because it's nice to see them and know they don't matter anymore.

On my desk is the little bamboo plant in the blue-swirly dish Melissa gave me for my last birthday, and my computer with the longest, hardest-to-spell password I could think of: "anthropological." That's so David won't figure it out. Across one bookshelf is a row of art supplies in cans: pencils, markers, and paintbrushes. On the next shelf are paint bottles and stacks of paper, everything from thick watercolor paper to filmy sheets of jewel-colored tissue paper. And lots of things I've collected: shells, rocks, a tiny glass elephant, a blackened old skeleton key my grandmother found in a chest but which unlocks nothing. I kept it because I like how it feels in my hand, the heart shape of the top and the jagged teeth at the bottom, and because —

Not everything worth keeping has to be useful.

Between my desk and my bed is a long window with gauzy purple curtains that let daylight through, even when the curtains are closed, and on the windowsill is a row of tiny colored bottles I bought one day at Elliot's Antiques: sunlit purple, green, and gold.

On the other side of my desk hangs my bulletin board, covered with drawings and little paintings: a pencil-gray castle I started but never finished, a monkey painted on an emerald tissue-paper rain forest, a colored-pencil cartoon from three years ago of my guinea pigs dancing — I still like it, even if it's old and I can do better now.

Well, there's something. I pick up my pencil and write on the first cards:

Drawing.

Guinea pig.

Under my window, Nutmeg and Cinnamon purr happily, shuffling through the shavings in their cage. Nutmeg lifts her head, and I look away quick.

Anytime they catch me watching them, my guinea pigs think I should feed them.

Picking up the next card, I decide I shouldn't do just "me" words. That day with the guitar, Jason could've used something fiery to say. Something juicier than "sad" or "mad." A string of words pop to mind, but I don't want to get in trouble with his mother. So I choose:

Gross!

Awesome!

Stinks a big one!!!

I'm not going to show these to Mom — especially the last one. I don't remember seeing exclamation points on any of Jason's other cards, but "awesome" with a period doesn't seem right. And if "gross" has one exclamation point, "stinks a big one" needs at least three.

My pen hovers over the sixth card. I could do

another favorite: "raspberry sherbet" or "ice-skating" or "goldfish." I look past my messy closet —

Open closet doors carefully. Sometimes things fall out.

— to the CDs, cassettes, and books lining the shelves near my bed. But Jason already has "book" and "music," and who knows if he even *likes* raspberry sherbet.

I could pick words about the clinic: "hallway" or "bookshelf" or "magazine." Or I could do funny words like "hoity-toity" or angry ones like "Oh, YEAH?" or hurt words like "I didn't mean to."

There's a gazillion words and phrases I could choose, and none of them seem worth one of my two last cards.

So I push the blank cards aside and draw pictures for the others. Drawing a guinea pig is easy. I sketch an oval, fat and compact, add black eyes, tiny rounded ears, tucked-under feet, and a mess of every-which-way hair. A furry baked potato.

The other words are harder. What does "awesome" look like? A smiley face? A sunrise? A double hot-fudge sundae?

My door creaks open a couple inches. A brown eye peeks through the crack.

David never remembers to knock. It irritates me so much I taped this rule right above my doorknob.

This is Catherine's room. David must knock!

"No toys in the fish tank," he says.

I pull forward one of my two blank cards and write in big block letters an unbendable, sharp-cornered David-word:

RULE.

By the time I get to the living room, David's already crouched in front of the fish tank, his smiling face reflected in the glass. Out the window behind the aquarium, I see Mom in the yard talking to the mailman.

And in the fish tank, one of my old Barbie dolls sits

on the gravel, her arm raised in a friendly wave, as though she's spotted Ken across the living room and is inviting him to join her.

And don't forget the scuba equipment, darling!

Barbie's pink-lipstick smile beams through the water, her long hair floating around her like a tangle of white-blond kelp. The goldfish nibble at it, and Barbie, Queen of the Fishes, waves cheerfully.

The goldfish are used to David dropping strange beings into their tank. They always swim over to check out the newest arrival and try to eat it. When that doesn't work, they accept it, along with their usual plastic plants and little castle.

"Remember the rule." I flip open the top of the aquarium. "No toys in the fish tank."

David nods, but I'm not fooled. He may not buy into the fish tank rule, but he's got this one down pat:

If you want someone to leave you alone, agree with her.

"You can only put things in here that belong," I

explain. "Like stuff you buy at a pet store. That's all that goes in the fish tank."

David leans in for a closer view as I pull Barbie up through the water. "'"Will power is trying hard *not* to do something that you really want to do," said Frog.'" He glances to me, hopeful.

Mom says David'll never learn to talk right if we keep letting him borrow words, but his face is so full of *please?* I say, "'"You mean like trying not to eat all of these cookies?" asked Toad.'"

Water from Barbie's hair trickles down my arm as I hold her over the fish tank, waiting for the dripping to stop.

Through the window, I notice Mom's gone and the girl next door is in her yard with Ryan Deschaine. He points at my house, and the girl spins around.

She waves.

I drop Barbie to wave back.

"No toys in the fish tank!" David cries. "It's wet!"

"It's okay," I say out of the corner of my smile. "It was an accident. I'll get her back out."

Ryan keeps talking, his hands moving like he's

explaining something. I hope he isn't saying things about me — especially not how I yelled at him when he called David a retard on the bus.

But her wave didn't seem like a making-fun wave, it seemed more of a "hi."

"Wet!"

Glancing to David, I see his pants wadded at his feet. I jump in front of the window to pull the curtains closed. "David, go find Mom. Now!"

I have a pants rule, too.

Pantless brothers are not my problem.

Sometimes things work out, but don't count on it.

On Saturday I find Mom in the kitchen pressing raw hamburger into patties. "I was thinking we should invite the new neighbors to our barbeque," she says. "This could be a nice chance to introduce ourselves."

"Great!" I watch her hands shape another hamburger and know I'd better choose my next words carefully. "What about David?"

"What about him?"

"Sometimes he forgets the rule about chewing with his mouth closed or he drinks from someone else's soda. Or —"

"They live next door, Catherine." Mom looks over the top of her glasses at me. "You can't pretend he doesn't exist."

I trace a line on the linoleum with my toe. "I know but it's hard enough to make new friends without worrying he'll do something embarrassing. I just want it to be nice today, a fun cookout with nothing going wrong."

"Dad and I'll watch him."

That's actually the worst possible answer. It's only a teeny step from both parents watching to neither watching — each thinking the other's in charge. "Maybe you could make a schedule? And take turns?"

"We'll both watch him." She pounds the hamburger with the palm of her left hand to flatten it. "Why don't you run over and invite the neighbors now, so I'll know how much food to prepare?"

"What time should I say?"

"Tell them lunch will be at one, though they're welcome to come early." She tears waxed paper from the roll and covers the layer of hamburgers.

Heading for the hallway, I remember what I came into the kitchen to ask. "Can we go to the mall later? I need some new colored pencils. My crimson and indigo are only about two inches long now, and I'd love more greens."

"Maybe you could earn them by doing extra baby-sitting?"

I grit my teeth to keep from snapping, "If David wanted them, you'd buy them." But there's no point, because I already know her answer: "That's different."

She's right. It *is* different and here's how: Everyone expects a tiny bit from him and a huge lot from me.

In the hallway I bounce between worrying things could go wrong (what if David spills something on his shorts and takes them off in front of everyone?) and hoping things go right (the girl next door might really like me). Before I open the front door, I close my eyes and wish: *Just this once, let it be easy.*

Outside, Dad is pitching a tennis ball to David on the front lawn. "Here it comes!"

David swings too late and the ball thumps against the side of the porch. "All done? Let's watch TV?"

"Like I said, you have to try ten times before you can watch TV." Dad picks another tennis ball from the pile on the grass at his feet. "We have five balls left. Catherine, tell him when to swing."

David and I sigh together. He lifts the plastic bat and moves his feet apart.

"Swing!" I yell as the ball comes close.

David misses anyway. "You need a bigger ball," I tell Dad. "He'd have a better chance."

"It'd help if we had a catcher," he replies. "Want to play?"

I look across the fence pickets to the woman in her lawn chair, reading. "No, thanks. Mom said I could invite the family next door to our cookout, and she's waiting to hear if they're coming."

Dad bends to grab the next ball from the pile.

"And you'll be in charge of David." It's only half the truth, but if Dad thinks he's in charge, he won't wait for Mom to do something.

"All right," he says. "Elbows up. Get ready to swing, David."

Walking to the fence, I notice the woman is younger than Mom, with short, brown hair and sunglasses so dark I can't see her eyes. "Excuse me?"

She sets her paperback facedown on her lap. "Hello."

"Hi. I live next door." I cringe at how stupid I sound. Of course I live next door! Why else would I be talking over our fence to her?

She smiles. "My daughter, Kristi, will be excited to meet you. She's with her dad this weekend, but I'll send her over to introduce herself when she gets back."

My heart drops. She's not home. "That'd be great. My mom was wondering —?"

David shrieks.

I turn to see the plastic bat flying through the air. David runs in a tight circle, flailing his arms, his mouth wide in another ear piercing howl.

As Mom dashes down the porch steps, Dad calls to her, "It's all right! It's just a bee."

I can't see our new neighbor's eyes behind her sunglasses, but her lips aren't smiling. I want to sink behind the fence and hide, but it wouldn't do any good. She'd still see me between the slats. "Oh, look at the time," I say, checking my watch. "Sorry, gotta go."

“’Bye,” the woman says. “I’ll tell Kristi you stopped over.”

Hurrying for the house, I pass Mom sitting cross-legged on the grass with David thrashing in her arms. David’s so big he doesn’t fit on Mom’s lap anymore, and they look twisted, an awkward tangle of elbows and knees, arms and legs.

Dad picks up the plastic bat. “Don’t baby him,” he says to Mom. “The bee didn’t even land on him.”

His back already to her, Dad doesn’t see Mom’s lowered eyebrows.

“He can’t help being afraid!” she snaps. “Why can’t *you* comfort him? It shouldn’t always have to be me.”

“You’re the one who ran out of the house!” Dad shoots back.

I glance to the fence, hoping the lady next door can’t hear them. She’s reading, her book held high to block the sun.

“Shh,” Mom soothes David. “It’s all right. A bee won’t hurt you unless you bother him.”

I want to yell at her, “It’s not that easy!” David

can't even figure out what'll bother *me*. I kick a tennis ball out of my way and watch it skitter across the grass and bounce against the steps.

Dad bends to pick up the tennis ball. As I run up the porch steps, he asks wearily, "Did you invite our new neighbors?"

"They're busy," I lie, closing the front door behind me.

Saying you'll do something means you have to do it – unless you have a very good excuse.

In front of me, Mom holds David's hand as we walk up the ramp to the clinic. "It's warm enough for the park today," I say, glancing across the parking lot to the strip of sun-sparkled ocean gleaming between Coastal Marine Supply and Otis's Hardware. "After I give Jason his words, can we go?"

"If David's doing well," Mom says.

I watch the back of David's head and repeat in my mind: *Do well today. Do well today.*

Inside, I sit on the waiting room couch, watching out the window. As soon as I see Jason's mother's van drive into the parking lot, I unload my backpack: word cards, sketchbook, colored pencils, CD player, and headphones.

"If you hadn't insisted on changing your shirt, we wouldn't be late," Mrs. Morehouse says, pushing Jason's wheelchair into the waiting room. "And I had to stop for gas."

"Hi, Jason." I hold the cards secret between my palms, waiting while his mother moves his wheelchair up beside me. She walks over to her regular chair near Mrs. Frost, settling in with a magazine.

I whisper to Jason, "I picked some words about me, and a few words I thought you should have."

But when I open my hands, Awesome! seems too flashy and bold for his book, and I feel silly for bringing it.

Jason looks at me, ready.

I wince, sliding the card into an empty pocket in his communication book. "I drew fireworks, but my first choice for 'awesome' would've been this." I offer my CD player to him.

Jason doesn't take it. He sits there, his Adam's apple rolling as he swallows. Help. On.

I flash a look to his mother. "It isn't far," she's saying to Mrs. Frost. "Forty minutes or so."

Maybe I can do this myself? I pull the headphones wide, hoping to drop them over Jason's ears, but as my hands come close, his hair tickles the underside of my wrist and surrounds my fingers. I hold my breath to keep from yanking my hands away as I position the headphones. Placing the CD player on his communication book, I push PLAY.

Jason startles.

"Sorry!" I roll the volume way down.

Music. Loud. More.

"Everything all right, Catherine?" Mrs. Morehouse asks.

"I think so." I roll the volume up until faint, stringy guitar music slips past the headphones into the waiting room.

Jason's jaw tightens. Like. Guitar.

"Me, too." I don't know if he can hear me with the headphones on, so I find Me, too. in his book and tap it.

Jason's head sways slightly to the music.

Waiting for the song to finish, I run my thumb along an edge of my word cards. Mom talks to

Carol, the receptionist explains something on the phone, and Jason's mother and Mrs. Frost discuss good restaurants that accommodate wheelchairs. Outside, a family wearing bright sweatshirts walks by the window, the father stopping to take a picture.

Tourists! I check my watch. If I hurry, Mom and I'll still have time to go to the park.

I feel a nudge on my arm.

"Oh." I hadn't noticed the song was over. Sliding my index finger under the top of the headphones, I pull gently. "See that tourist family out the window?" I ask, putting my CD player away. "I think they're a good-luck sign that summer's here." I hunt through my stack of cards to find the word I want good luck for the most. The last card I made, the one with a drawing of a girl's hand raised in a "hi" wave. Friend.

"I have a new neighbor who's my age," I say. "I haven't met her yet, but I'm hoping she's nice."

He smiles. Catherine. Friend.

"I do have friends — my best friend is Melissa — but no one that lives near me. My neighborhood is mostly old people and families with little kids. Well, except the boy who lives on the corner. He's my age, but he —" Stinks a big one!!!

I put that card as far from my name as possible. "You'll have to be careful when you use this one. The last time I yelled this, I had to sit in the front seat of the bus."

No. I mean. Catherine. My. Friend.

My lips feel dry. I lick them, though Mom always tells me not to. "Sure," I say, even if I think of us more as clinic friends than always friends. Seeing Jason's finger on the word, I wonder why he didn't already have it.

"And this is a guinea pig." I wait for his hand to move. "I have two of these at home. Their names are Cinnamon and Nutmeg, and I'll put 'guinea pig' right here next to 'sandwich,' because eating is what they like best." I slide the card into the pocket. "And I thought you might want 'gross.' This lady I drew is eating cereal. But do you see this white thing on the spoon? It's a maggot."

Jason curls his upper lip.

"It's even worse, because it's *half* a maggot!" I add the card to his book. "And this word I picked for my brother, David."

My other cards have the word printed small at the top, but the tall block letters of RULE. fill the card. "David loves rules, so I use those to teach him."

What? RULE.

I usually don't share my rule collection with anyone but David, but Jason's different. "David doesn't learn from watching other people, so I have to teach him everything." I open my sketchbook to my Rules for David, figuring it's easier to show than explain.

Take your shoes off at the doctor, but at the dentist leave them on.

If you want to get out of answering something, pretend you didn't hear.

If someone is holding something you want, ask if you can have a turn.

"David has his own rules, too," I say, "but those rules don't make sense to anyone but him."

What? Those. RULE.

I sigh. "David's got lots. One is, the cellar door always has to be shut. Even if I'm only going downstairs to grab something, he'll race over and shut the door. Once he even locked it and I got stuck down there with a whole bunch of spiders until Mom heard me yelling.

"And the worst part, it's not just our house. David'll hunt through *other people's* houses, too." I can't help seeing it in my mind: David running down Melissa's hallway, and Melissa's mother saying kindly, "Don't worry, Catherine, it's fine. David, that's the closet. That's the bathroom."

Jason nods. Brother. Me, too. Matt.

"Is he younger than you?"

No. Five. Years. Older.

"Oh, you're lucky then! You never have to babysit." As soon as the words leave my mouth, I want to swallow them back. Of course he couldn't babysit. "Um."

When you say something stupid, gloss over it with superfast talking and maybe no one'll notice.

"The next word is 'drawing.' I picked it because it's one of my favorite things to do." Looking for a good empty pocket, it hits me — he can't draw.

But Jason's already seen the word, so there's nothing to do but slide the card into a pocket beneath my name.

What? Guinea pig. Eat.

"Huh?"

What? Guinea pig. Jason waits for me to say each word before he taps the next. Eat.

"What do guinea pigs eat?"

Yes.

"Oh. Mostly they eat pellets from the pet store, but they'll eat almost anything. Once I left a library book too close to their cage and they ate off half the cover. That was hard to explain to the librarian, let me tell you."

Jason laughs, a sharp bark like a Canada goose. His mother looks up from her magazine as I scan the room and see everyone watching us.

"Uh, but I think carrots are their favorite." I lean away from Jason. "They can hear me snap a carrot all the way from the kitchen."

Jason closes his lips tight. Thank you. Catherine. New. Words.

"No problem." I stare at the rows of plain, black-and-white cards and wish that all his cards were colorful. "Would you like me to make more?"

Awesome! Tell. Mom.

"Excuse me, Mrs. Morehouse? Jason wants me to make him more words."

She walks over, and I watch her eyebrows go up as her gaze sweeps Jason's book. "How many cards would you like?" she asks.

I don't know where my voice comes from, but it says, "All of them."

She looks surprised but hands me the whole stack. When she's settled back with her magazine, I slide the blank cards into my shorts pocket. "I'm sorry I drew you that day," I whisper to Jason.

Don't. Like. Picture. Me.

"I didn't mean any —"

"HI, JASON!"

For the first time, I'm sorry to see his speech therapist stride into the waiting room.

"How's his day been going?" she asks his mother.

"Wonderful," Mrs. Morehouse says. "In fact, he was so anxious to come to speech today, he even changed his shirt for you."

"How nice!" the therapist says. "WE DO HAVE FUN" (two fingers tapping her nose then swinging down to her other hand) "DON'T WE?" (cheesy grin).

Jason sneaks his hand over his cards. Speech. Woman. Stinks a big one!!!

I nod and tap, Very much.

As his therapist pushes his wheelchair toward the corridor, Jason glances back to me.

"See you Thursday," I say.

His therapist's voice grows softer the farther she goes. I turn to my rule collection and add:

Some people think they know who you are, when really they don't.

If you can only choose one, pick carefully.

On Wednesday morning the minivan is gone from the driveway next door, so I busy myself collecting words and phrases for Jason in the blank spaces of my sketchbook. Words from commercials, conversations, and books run between my doodles and across the backs of my drawings. The driveway remains empty until after dark.

An hour before OT on Thursday, I lay my sketchbook open on my desk and flip the pages, hunting for the right words and phrases to put on Jason's cards.

Why not?

He already has "why," but "why not" is pushier — like "why" with a fist on its hip.

Out my window I see the minivan still parked

next door. Why not? Because Mom's calling clients and Dad's at work so David's my responsibility — that's why.

"Just for an hour," Mom said, "until we have to leave for OT. I've put on a Thomas the Tank Engine video so he shouldn't be any trouble."

I pull forward two blank cards and scrawl:

Yeah, right.

Whatever.

I know she needs me to babysit sometimes, but I hate when she tells me he shouldn't be any trouble. Trouble comes quick with David, and "should" doesn't have anything to do with it. He should remember to flush the toilet, too, but that doesn't mean it happens.

When Mom had gone, I took my long mirror off my door and propped it at an angle against one corner of the living room, so I could work at my desk and still see David reflected in the mirror.

Every few words I make, I glance out my bedroom doorway to the mirror. David stands at the TV, the remote in his hand. He loves rewinding the trains backward up the tracks and speeding them ahead to almost crashing, over and over.

I turn another sketchbook page and choose among the words written along the edge. Sure. You bet! Excellent! Perfect. Frustrating. Pretty. and Dazzling! to jazz up and stretch the words Jason has in bigger directions, and Joke. so he can be sarcastic if he wants.

I peek toward the mirror. The TV train steams ahead, billowing smoke, toward the shed. "Watch out!" David repeats, a perfect imitation of the narrator's voice.

But at the last second possible before the smash, David hits PAUSE. Jumping in front of the frozen TV picture, he waves the remote in circles, like it's a magic wand.

Watch Out!!!

On the next page is my half-finished portrait of Jason. I pick up a pencil and add the details I couldn't add in the waiting room: eyelashes, thick eyebrows, and the outline of his thin lips. Part of me wishes I could tear this picture out of my sketchbook and crumple it into a tight ball so I don't hear his mother's scolding in my head when I see it, but the rest of me is bothered that it's —

Incomplete. Too much like a Secret.

"Are you busy?" a girl's voice asks.

I drop my pencil and flash a look from my unmade bed to the folded clothes piled on my bureau. Cinnamon and Nutmeg crane their necks to *wheek* at Mom and the girl from next door standing in my doorway.

"I saw Kristi coming up the walk," Mom says, smiling. "Catherine, I have one more call to make. Could you keep an eye on David for a few more minutes? Then I'll take over, I promise."

Before I can get out "no," I see Mom's legs in the mirror, hurrying back toward her office. David pushes REWIND, and Thomas speeds backward again.

"Come in!" I offer my chair, but Kristi sits on the edge of my desk, crossing her feet at the ankles.

"Are you busy?" she asks.

"No!" Seeing her up close, I know Kristi will be popular. Not only for her straight brown hair, parted off-center, shining down to her elbows. Or because she looks just right, even wearing frayed jean shorts and a T-shirt. Kristi radiates "cool," and I know it as sure as I know David'll stop that speeding train at the last-last second.

Part of me feels sorry, because she doesn't look like a flashlights-and-Morse-code kid, but the other part of me is excited.

"I'm glad Mrs. Bowman sold you her house," I say. "Well, I guess, technically, *the realtor* sold it, but I'm glad your family bought it, because I've always thought it would be great if a kid lived next door. Mrs. Bowman was nice, but she was really, really old." I clamp my teeth together to keep anything else dumb from escaping my mouth.

Kristi drags a strand of her hair between her fingers. "I'm glad, too. I was scared I'd have to start school next year without knowing *anyone*."

My lips spread to a smile imagining Melissa's surprise as I introduce Kristi into our group. "This is my friend Kristi," I'll say. "We hung out together all summer."

I glance out my doorway to the living room. Where's David?

"Ryan said there's a bus stop at the end of the street?"

I lick my bottom lip to keep from grimacing. "At the corner."

"That's great." Kristi continues to twist her strand of hair. "I used to walk three blocks to catch the bus — even when it was freezing or raining. Mom'd say, 'Take the umbrella,' as though anyone carries an umbrella!"

David insists on bringing his bright red umbrella to school even when it's only cloudy. "My mom's like that, too."

Leaving out isn't the same as lying.

"She always says, 'Well, at least wear your hood!'" I continue, "Like I'd want hood hair."

Kristi smiles, letting the twisted strand fall back to her arm. "Ryan said he lets kids wait in his house when it's raining, since he can see the bus come from there."

But only if you're invited. I peek out the doorway into the empty living room. Part of me would like to tell Kristi the truth, but I don't want our conversation to become about David.

At the bus stop I always tell him, "You have your umbrella," grabbing the back of his jacket to keep him from following Ryan's friends up the steps. "Going inside is for kids without umbrellas." I would be honest, but David doesn't understand invited and not invited. He thinks everything is for everyone.

"Ryan's nice," Kristi says. "Don't you think so?"

Nice as a cockroach. "Want some sherbet?" I ask.

When you want to get out of answering something, distract the questioner with another question.

"What kind?" Kristi asks.

"Raspberry."

David rushes through my doorway, his eyes wide with panic, an audiocassette in his hand. "Fix it?"

The tape has pulled out of the cassette, hanging in a long, delicate loop.

At first I'm relieved that's all that's wrong until my guinea pigs start to squeal.

With the cassette over one ear, and his hand shielding the other, David yells, "Quiet, pigs!"

Kristi shoots a worried glance from David to the guinea pigs to me.

I pry the cassette from David's fingers, knowing it'll be faster to deal with the tape than the tears filling his eyes. "Don't worry. This'll only take a minute."

I spin the cassette around and around on my finger, wishing I had two more hands: one to give the guinea pigs hay to quiet them, another to cover David's mouth as he shrieks. I spin the cassette so fast my finger keeps slipping out of the tiny hole.

When the tape lies flat and tight, I slide *Frog and Toad Together* into my cassette player and push PLAY. Arnold Lobel's deep voice joins the guinea pig squeals, and David's face lights up like Christmas morning, Halloween night, and his birthday, all rolled into one big grin. "You fixed it!"

"Go find Mom," I say, pressing the cassette into his hand, "and tell her I'm done babysitting." Before I close the door, I peek into the living room to be sure David's heading toward Mom's office. He disappears down the hallway, swinging his arms.

"That must be hard," Kristi says. "Even regular little brothers are a pain."

"Regular" snarls in my stomach. I grab my sticky notes and write "DAD! Buy a new tape player!" and stick it on the back of my door to remember to tell him — again.

To quiet my guinea pigs, I pull strings of timothy hay from the little bale I keep under the cage. Nutmeg yips as Cinnamon steals her hay.

"They're so cute," Kristi says. "Can I hold them?"

"Sure." I toss her a towel. "Better put that on your lap, in case they pee." I slide one hand under Nutmeg's chest and cup her back legs with my other.

Cinnamon *wheeks* until I set her next to Nutmeg on Kristi's lap, and the squealing turns to happy-pig cooing:

Nutmeg, I thought I'd never see you again! Say, what are you eating?

Towel, medium rare, with a hint of fabric softener. Care for a bite?

Don't mind if I do!

My door bursts open. "No toys in the fish tank," David announces.

"I'll be right back," I say to Kristi between my clenched teeth.

"No problem," she says, stroking Nutmeg's neck.

I close my door behind me so Kristi won't see me run. "Why?" I sprint ahead of David. "Why today?"

"Because."

A tiny cowboy stands bowlegged on the gravel at the bottom of the fish tank, one hand poised to grab his pistol, the other holding the end of a lasso hovering in a loop above his head. A goldfish swims right through the hole.

Git back here, ya pesky varmint!

Plunging my hand into the water, fish swoosh past my fingers. I rescue the cowboy and throw him into the toy box. Grabbing David's wrist, I don't even wipe my hand first.

"Wet!" David twists to get away.

"You're not going to ruin this for me." I yank him along behind me down the hallway to Mom's office.

She's on the phone. "All right, then," Mom says into the receiver. "I'll look forward to hearing from you next week."

"I have company," I say, not caring about interrupting her, "and you need to watch David."

Mom holds up one finger for me to wait, but I push David ahead of me into the room. Her eyebrows come down.

She grabs a puzzle off her bookshelf and dumps the pieces on the floor. "Yes, that'll be fine," she says into the phone.

David sits beside the hill of pieces. He can't stand to see puzzles undone, but he insists on doing the pieces in lines, like he's reading the puzzle. He doesn't look for all the red barn pieces or the daisies in the field or the glimmers of sunlit water. Left to right, top to bottom, that's his puzzle rule. And if you add a piece out of David's order, he'll take it back out — even if it fits.

I slam Mom's office door on my way out.

When I come back to my room, breathless from

running down the hallway, I notice Nutmeg and Cinnamon are in their cage again.

"Everything okay?" Kristi asks. "I hope you don't mind that I looked at this."

She's holding my sketchbook, open to the half-finished portrait of Jason. "Is he your boyfriend?"

"No! Just a boy I started drawing."

Kristi tilts her head in an oooh-really? look.

If you want someone to think something's not important, use "just" a lot.

"He's just a boy I know from — well, I don't really know him. Not very well. I just see him at —" I check my watch. It's almost time to leave for OT.

I can't tell Kristi I have to go — not the first time we've met. But I told Jason I'd see him today.

Kristi tosses my sketchbook onto my desk. My hands itch to flip the page, but that'll bring attention to it.

"Want to watch TV?" Kristi asks.

If I say no, maybe I won't get another chance to hang out with her. I glance to Thomas the Tank Engine reflected in my mirror, his eyes closed, braced for a crash that'll never happen. From somewhere, David shrieks.

"We could watch at my house," Kristi says.

That stings, even if I agree. "Sure," I say. "I'll tell my mom."

All the way up Kristi's walkway, I want to skip or run or twirl with my arms out, like a six-year-old. It feels deliciously easy to be visiting a friend's house without having to say first, "Sorry, David, this is for me. You can't come."

Hearing Mom's car back out of the driveway, I turn to wave. She waves, but David sits alone in the backseat, hunched down, his hands over his ears.

I follow Kristi up the steps and through her front door.

At someone else's house, you have to follow their rules.

At a friend's house, everything is uncomplicated. No one drops toys in the fish tank, no one cares if the cellar door is open or closed, and no one shrieks unless there's a huge, hairy spider crawling up her arm.

And they only have regular family rules:

No snacks right before supper.

Call if you're going to be late.

Homework first.

But the best part of being at a friend's house is I can be just me and put the sister part of me down.

Kristi's room looks like a page from a catalog, the sort of shiny catalog I get in the mail and can only afford a toothbrush or a poster from. But Kristi's new pink-swirled curtains match the fat comforter on her bed, which matches the pink-and-blue rug on her floor.

It's all beautiful, but what I envy most is the neat row of things on her bureau. Photographs, makeup, her jewelry tree, and a long row of nail-polish bottles — everything out in the open, not jumbled in drawers like mine, out of David's sight.

Lying next to Kristi on her new-smelling pink comforter, I wish I wasn't wearing an old, sun-faded T-shirt and had put on makeup this morning.

"I think he's cute," Kristi says, and I force my gaze back to the *Teen People* spread in front of us. The boy in the magazine has perfect teeth and stabbing dark eyes.

Kristi taps the little box that says UP CLOSE AND PERSONAL WITH JAKE. "He says his ideal date would be a sunset walk on the beach and a picnic supper she had prepared."

"He sounds cheap." Soon as I say it, I wish I could stuff the words back into my mouth.

But Kristi laughs. "Yeah. Why can't *he* bring the picnic? If you get invited somewhere, you shouldn't have to bring supper!" She flips onto her back.

I roll over, too. Her ceiling is ordinary, plain white with a simple, square glass light in the middle and two hooks, like upside-down question marks, holding nothing. I think Mrs. Bowman hung plants here.

"Can you date yet?" Kristi asks.

I shrug. "I know boys from school and church, but no one I'd want to go somewhere with — by myself. Well, not *really* by myself, because he'd be there, too." Oh, shut up, I tell my tongue.

"You should ask that boy you drew on a date," Kristi says. "What's his name?"

I shift my shoulders, pretending I need to stretch so she won't notice I'm squirming. Is there any harm in telling his name? They're not likely to meet. Jason doesn't even go to the same school I do.

"Jason."

"My boyfriend and I broke up before I moved,"

Kristi says. "But I think Ryan likes me. His mom works at the community center where I volunteer. Did you know the community center is sponsoring a summer dance? It's for kids aged eight to seventeen. You could ask Jason."

"You volunteer?" I need to change the subject.

"Yeah, with the preschool day camp. It sounded fun when I signed up, but they want me to come every day now. And with going to Dad's every weekend, I haven't even had time to finish unpacking."

I glance to her bureau, to the framed photograph of a man standing with a dog. "My friend Melissa's parents are divorced. She's in California for the summer with her dad."

"My parents aren't divorced."

She says it so sharp, I gasp. "I'm sorry, I thought because —"

"They're just separated." Kristi reaches up to twirl a piece of hair in her fingers. "They're just taking a break for a while."

It's so quiet I can hear birds outside and cars driving past on the road. Kristi holds the very end of the lock of hair and it spins back, falling against the path of freckles across her nose.

"Want to shoot some baskets?" she asks, pushing her hair away. "I don't know which box my basketball's in, but it's in the garage somewhere."

"Sure."

I can't help checking off a list of differences in each room we pass through. No locks on the doors, no little-kid videos next to the TV, no safety plugs in the outlets, and a box of cookies left out on the kitchen table — no one worried someone will eat them all at once.

Kristi's garage is full of boxes, bikes, rakes, a snowblower, and a clutter of other things. We open boxes until we find her basketball. "I hope you're not real good." Kristi passes me the ball. "I'm only kinda good."

"Me, too," I say, relieved. We play one-on-one, until I see Dad pull into our driveway with David.

David runs up the walkway to our house, clutching his video.

"Hi!" Dad smiles, coming toward the fence. "It's a nice surprise to drive in and see you next door, Cath."

First, I've told him not to call me "Cath," because it sounds too much like he's calling me a baby cow, and second, why's it such a surprise I have a friend next door?

"You need to get David a new tape player." I set up for a shot. "The one he has keeps pulling his cassettes apart, and I have to fix them." The ball bounces off the rim.

"Can't you say 'hello' first?" Dad asks.

"Hello. But don't forget. I'm sick of fixing his cassettes."

"I'm Catherine's dad." He nods to Kristi. "It's nice to have you and your family in the neighborhood. What do your parents —?"

"Oh, wow." I check my watch. "It's getting late."

"Yeah, I have to start supper for my mom." Kristi shoots the ball. "I'll see you?"

"Definitely!" I get the ball and pass it to her, loving the hollow *thump* it makes hitting her hands.

"I'll be in in a minute," Dad calls. "I need to get something from the car."

I walk home, easy as you please. In the living room,

I can barely keep from skipping past Mom reading the newspaper on the couch. Next to her David shakes his hands with excitement as a video preview plays on the TV.

"Did you have fun?" Mom asks me. The newspaper pages make a whispery sound as she folds them. "Kristi seems like a nice girl."

I nod.

David slaps his legs with his hands. "Rated PG for adventure, action, and peril!"

"Jason missed you today," Mom says, and my happiness deflates like a balloon with the smallest tear.

"He said that?"

"Well, actually, what he said was, 'Tell Catherine all gone stinks a big one.'" Mom looks over the top of her glasses, giving the long, what-have-you-been-up-to-young-lady? stare.

"Who's Jason?" Dad says from the doorway, a teasing smirk on his face.

"A boy at David's OT place." I watch Dad's eyebrows shoot upward, and I roll my eyes. "He's just a boy. It's not like he's a *boy* or anything."

"Oh, I almost forgot, Jason sent you something," Mom says. "It's in a bag on the kitchen table."

"PG-thirteen," David shouts. "Parents strongly cautioned!"

I stroll, ho-hum, to the kitchen but I'm curious. On the table I find a paper bag and reach inside. My fingers touch something tickly, cold. I pull out a big bunch of carrots, the feathery green tops attached.

Untangling a carrot from the bunch, I imagine Cinnamon and Nutmeg in their cage, shuffling through the shavings, drinking from the water bottle.

I snap the carrot in half.

From down the hall comes a crazed burst of squealing. Then a shriek: "QUIET, PIGS!"

By the time I reach my room, David's standing in my doorway, his hands over his ears. "Sorry." I push past him. "Go back to your video. They'll stop in a minute."

Cinnamon and Nutmeg jostle each other, their front feet high against the side of the cage.

Out of my way, fatso!

Who are you calling fat, hairball? That carrot is mine!

I toss carrot bits into the cage, and a shaving-flying

scuffle breaks out, finally settling into happy chortling and chewing sounds.

A trickle of guilt curls through me. Why can't the world be simpler, like it is for guinea pigs? They only have a few rules:

Crying will get you attention.

If it fits in your mouth, it's food.

Scream if you don't get your share.

But I can make it up to Jason on Tuesday.

I already know how.

If it fits in your mouth, it's food.

Tuesday I bring something to the clinic I've never brought before. Something that means I need to leave the top of my backpack unzipped, and instead of swinging it to my shoulder, I carry it gingerly in my arms.

Jason is already there when I arrive, his wheelchair parked next to my usual spot on the couch.

"Hi." I sit beside him, arranging my backpack on my lap. "Thanks for the carrots."

Did? Guinea pig. Like.

"They thought they were awesome. In fact —" I pull my backpack zipper all the way down.

A furry, eager face pops out. *What's up? And more to the point, what's for lunch? Pellets? Carrots? Ooh, is that carpeting down there?*

"This is Nutmeg," I say, cradling her against my chest. "And she says, 'Thanks for the carrots.'" Nutmeg has chocolate-brown whorls of fur, glossy black eyes, and a friendly personality. Of my two guinea pigs, I figured she'd be more tolerant of Jason's sudden movements and noises.

Jason's mouth hangs slack.

"Would you like to pet her?" I ask. "She might squeal, but she doesn't bite."

Awesome!

Nutmeg walks across Jason's communication book. She sniffs the air and poops on Van.

"Sorry!" I jump to grab a tissue from the box on the receptionist's desk. "Nutmeg! What kind of 'hello' is that?"

Gross! Hello.

I clean Jason's book. "You can say that again."

Gross! Hello.

"Very funny." I reach into the front pocket of my backpack. "Speaking of jokes, I made words for you."

When I look up, Jason is stroking Nutmeg's back with his fingertips. I can see by the clench of Jason's jaw how hard he's struggling to control his movements to not frighten her. When he brings his hand away, he's trembling.

I pretend not to notice, afraid it'll embarrass him. "This first card is 'joke.' I thought you could use this word when you're telling a joke or being sarcastic, to make sure the other person knows you're kidding."

Like. Word.

"And this is 'whatever.'" I lean over to whisper, "It's good for annoying your mother; at least, it has that effect on mine." I demonstrate, swinging my gaze to the ceiling. "Whatever."

Jason grins. Good job. Whatever.

I move Nutmeg over so I can slide the cards, word after word, in Jason's book. "And this is 'secret.' I thought sometimes we might want to talk without everyone hearing us. When one of us taps 'secret,' we'll switch to only using your cards. Want to try it?"

Yes.

I look around for something to talk about. Out the window a man hurries across the parking lot, his beagle on a leash. "Do you see that guy?" I ask, pointing. "Let's imagine who he is."

The man dashes past the windows. The beagle trots beside him, head down, sniffing.

Jason taps, Late. For. Dog. Show.

I give Jason a thumbs-up. Good job. My. Turn. I imagine the man and his dog as a perfect spy team, too ordinary to be noticed.

But Jason doesn't have "spy" or "secret agent" or even "mysterious." Searching Jason's book, Man. Is. A. Secret. is the best I can do.

"I was imagining them a secret agent team," I say finally. "Maybe we can talk about music, instead?"

Yes.

I pull my CD player from the front pocket of my backpack. "This is my favorite CD." Putting the headphones over Jason's ears isn't as awkward as last time, but I still fight the urge to shiver as his hair brushes my fingers and the backs of my hands.

Who? Music.

I check his book, but of course, there's no card. "It's —"

Jason taps, Secret.

I clamp my hand over my mouth. *Don't speak.*

Catherine. Make. Word. Who?

I don't have a blank card, so I remove Good-bye. from Jason's book and draw on the back. It's not a great picture of Avril Lavigne, but I'm in a hurry.

I don't bother to slide it in Jason's book, just lay the card on top. It's a temporary word, and he'll need "good-bye" more.

Jason studies the picture, headphones on, music playing. Avril Lavigne. Stupid.

"What?" I startle Nutmeg into skittering across Jason's book.

Jason grins. Joke.

I dip my head in my best imitation of Mom's no-nonsense look. "You think you're funny, don't you?" I lift one side of the headphones, so he'll hear me better. "My next card is going to say 'you big jerk.'"

Secret.

I spoke *again*! I bite my tongue to keep from using it and scan my word choices, lifting Nutmeg to see what she's sitting on.

Jason taps, Like. Avril Lavigne.

Me, too. is all I can find to say.

"HI, JASON!"

Jason scowls as I take the headphones off his ears. Speech. Woman. Yell. All the time. He taps. I. Can't. Talk. But. I. Hear. Fine.

"HI, JASON!" his therapist repeats, louder. "How's his day been going?" she asks his mother.

Jason's hand moves. Loud. Day.

"What a sweet little animal!" the speech therapist says. "But what's it doing?"

I glance at Nutmeg busy chewing the edge of Good-bye.

I lunge for her. "I'm sorry, Jason."

He smiles. od-bye. Guinea pig.

Watching his therapist push Jason's chair down the hallway, I hold Nutmeg against my chest, stroking her back with my fingertips. "Could we stop at the mall on the way home?" I ask Mom. "I need card stock and a paper cutter."

Jason needs so many words.

Sometimes people laugh when they like you.

But sometimes they laugh to hurt you.

On the ride home from the mall, Mom says, "I can't believe Nutmeg ate Jason's card."

I laugh with her, stroking Nutmeg huddled against my stomach. "She loves paper almost as much as carrots." I rub Nutmeg under her chin, right where she likes it best. She hates the rumbling of the car, and only my touch stops her from shaking.

I peek into the bag at my feet: a paper cutter, white card stock, and a tin of forty-eight colored pencils, twelve more than the set I have. "Thanks for the new colored pencils."

"You're welcome," Mom says. "I've seen you making words for Jason and you've been babysitting a lot lately."

I can't wait to get home and see those colors on the page: aquamarine, magenta, limepeel, peacock blue, and the others. And I won't have to limit using my crimson and indigo pencils anymore. Now I have brand-new long ones.

"Wouldn't you like to sign up for an art class?" Mom says. "I hate to see you spend your whole summer doing nothing."

I meet her gaze in the rearview mirror. "I'm doing things."

"Mrs. Deschaine tells me there's still time to register for yoga. Wouldn't that be fun? Or one of the bus trips?"

"I'll think about it."

Leaning my head against the side of the open car window, I pull in a long breath of warm clam flats. The tide is out, almost to the inner islands, and a lone man is digging clams. Far away he looks like a doll bent over his rake, a bucket at his feet.

Beside me David is asleep, his head dropped over almost to his shoulder as if trying to cover one ear. He gasps a tiny sound, wrinkling his nose, and I wonder if it's the clam flats he's smelling or if he's dreaming.

But I don't even know if David does dream — he's never told me.

"David's asleep," I say.

Mom glances in the rearview mirror, and her cheeks lift to a smile. "Stephanie must've tired him out."

Almost home, I see Ryan playing basketball with Kristi in her driveway. She waves, but that doesn't untie the knot in my stomach.

David wakes, stretching his legs long as he can, still wearing his seat belt. Kristi sets down the basketball and comes toward my yard, Ryan following.

"David," I say, "go inside with —"

Too late. Seat belt undone, he's already out of the car, running to meet Kristi and Ryan.

"I'll take Nutmeg and your things," Mom says. "Send David in if you go next door."

"But, Mom!"

"He doesn't have any friends — not like you have." She looks at me over her glasses. "Surely you can let David stay a few minutes?"

I'm torn between all losing choices. David will scream if I make him go inside now. Mom'll think

I'm selfish if I beg her to take him with her. Then there's Ryan.

I cross my arms and pick the one "maybe" choice. Maybe Ryan doesn't want to look bad in front of Kristi any more than I do.

"I'll be in my office," Mom says.

Ryan leans against our fence and blows a bubble with his gum.

"Gum?" David might not notice lots of things, but gum is something he never misses.

"Yeah, it's gum." Ryan pulls a piece from the pack in his hand and gives it to Kristi. He throws another at me.

My hand shoots up to catch the gum, before I can even decide if I want it.

"Can I have a turn?" David asks Ryan.

"I've been waiting for you to come home." Kristi unwraps her gum.

"I went to OT with David." I drop the gum in my shorts pocket. "Then I had to stop at the mall."

"Can I have a turn?" David asks again. "If someone is holding something you want, ask if you can have a turn. That's the rule."

"What's OT?" Kristi asks.

I don't want to explain, but both Kristi and Ryan are watching me. "Occupational therapy. David works on writing, jumping, stuff like that."

Ryan turns to David. "You can't jump?"

If we were at the bus stop, I'd already be yelling. But Kristi's forehead is creased in concern. "Of course, he can —"

"Jump!" Ryan says.

David jumps up and down.

"Stop it," I tell him.

Up and down, David jumps, staring at the pack of gum in Ryan's hand. Up and down.

"Stop!" I grab David's arm, but he won't stop jumping. He lands hard on my foot as I'm reaching into my pocket, fumbling for my piece of gum.

"Ryan, give him some gum," Kristi says.

"It's a miracle!" Ryan holds a piece of gum out to David. "You're cured!"

But when David opens the wrapper, there's nothing inside. He head-butts his face into my shirt. "It's gone!"

"You jerk!" I scream at Ryan so loud, David bursts into tears. "Get out of my yard and take your stupid gum with you."

"It was just a joke." Ryan pulls another piece of gum from his pack, but David has his arms wrapped so tight around me, he can't take it.

"He can have mine," I snap.

"We should go, Kris," Ryan says. "I have to get home."

"I'm sorry, Catherine," Kristi says, her face white. "I'll call you, okay?"

"Okay." I pull David up our porch steps and into the house, not stopping until the front door bangs closed behind me. "MOM!"

Through the window, I watch Ryan gesturing, like he's explaining something. Probably telling Kristi all the bad things I've ever said to him and leaving out all the reasons why.

Kristi nods, and that tiny "yes" bleeds the fight out of me.

"Gum?" David asks.

I study the hair on the top of his head. How can his

outside look so normal and his inside be so broken? Like an apple, red perfect on the outside, but mushy brown at the first bite.

"Can I have a turn?"

I pull the gum out of my pocket and put it on the perfect top of David's head.

He takes it off his hair. I watch him unwrap it and stuff the gum in his mouth, dropping the wrapper on the floor.

"Trash goes in the garbage can," I say. "That's the rule."

"I'm sorry, Frog."

I turn away, but David's hand holding the wrapper comes into my view. "I'm sorry, Frog?" he says, panic edging his voice.

David gets scared when people don't answer him, and the first tiny pinpricks poke me, little guilty jabs whispering, "He's doing the best he can."

And I brace myself for the *ka-boom*, sure to follow. The full guilt avalanche, thundering down the mountainside, sweeping away houses, knocking me flat.

I take the wrapper. "Okay, Toad."

"Catherine!" Mom says. "He needs to speak his own words, but he won't if you keep encouraging him to echo."

Unfairness punches me in the stomach. "You let him ruin everything!" I say. "It's always about him!"

"He needs more from me. Stop overreacting."

I run to my room, slamming my bedroom door so hard Nutmeg and Cinnamon dart to the far corner of their cage.

Grabbing my sketchbook, I flip to a blank page and write words, bearing down so hard the letters cut into the page.

'Unfair.' 'Cruel.' 'Hate.' 'Ruined.' 'Murky.' 'Tease.' 'Embarrassed.'

My hands tremble as I write. They shake so much, it doesn't look like my handwriting. I try to rob the words of their weight by concentrating on the letters. Nice, sharp T, round O.

'TORN.'

But I'm not fooling myself. I know the power these words hold. I drop my forehead on my arms.

My door creaks, but my head is too heavy to lift. "Go away," I say.

A cassette comes into the dark space between my arm and face. "I'm sorry, Frog," David says.

I do what will send him away. Around and around and around, I spin the cassette on my finger.

David leans against my arm.

"I wish it had been Kristi without Ryan," I say. "Everything would've been different. Or if Mom hadn't —"

"You fixed it!" David says.

I look down. The tape is wound tight again.

As it plays, I watch David's lips mouth the words, every pause, every word, perfectly in time with Arnold Lobel's voice. His fingers flicker, like blades of grass shivered by wind. Fluttering their own silent dance.

"Who are you?" I ask.

"I'm David," he says.

Open closet doors carefully. Sometimes things fall out.

As Mom reads, I sketch the scene: Harry sneaking down the hallway on a midnight search. I practice drawing perspective, angling the lines of the corridor narrower with each door to pass.

I imagine David turning the doorknobs, needing to know what's on the other side. Not even realizing the walls are squeezing in, tighter and tighter, the farther he walks.

I flip my page to save him.

Beside me, my word cards sit upside down on the waiting room couch, a tiny white pile. At home I felt ready to share these words, but what if Jason tells me I'm being selfish to feel bad for *me* when David — and he — has it worse?

"And how much for shipping?" the receptionist asks, the phone to her ear. "Is there any discount if we buy two boxes?"

I yank the zipper open on my backpack to find a blank card. Maybe I have time to make new words before Jason gets here.

"That does seem a lot for one box of hearing-aid batteries," the receptionist says.

I lay a card on my sketchbook, but before I can choose a word, Carol rushes through the clinic doorway, her baby balanced on her hip. "And there was *such* a line of traffic on the bridge!" she says over Jason's head to Mrs. Morehouse, behind her. "Figures they'd have to raise it for a ship on the day I'm already late."

Excuse. I write the word, quick as I can.

"That's always the way, isn't it?" Mrs. Morehouse pushes Jason's chair across the carpet toward me, and Mom picks up her bookmark, leaving Harry still searching in the hallway.

Jason smiles, his hair curling along his forehead and above his ears, no longer dangling past his eyebrows.

"Your haircut looks good." I slide my words pile under my leg.

Too. Short. He nods toward the card in my lap. What? Word.

I frown, sliding Excuse. into an empty pocket of his communication book. With no picture, the card looks rushed and cheap. My fingers itch to pull it out again. "I'm sorry," I say. "The rest of the words I brought aren't good words."

Want. Bad. Words.

"Not that kind of bad," I say, a grin sneaking out. "I mean I was upset when I wrote them. Maybe I could make double for next week?"

He shakes his head. Want. Those. Words.

I glance to Mom, but she doesn't look up from her magazine.

"And how soon can I expect delivery?" the receptionist asks into the phone. "Maine."

Jason stares at me, touching an empty pocket in his book, his finger tapping a soft drumbeat.

I pull a card from under my leg. Not even looking

at what it is, I reach across and slide the word into a pocket of Jason's communication book. Murky.

What? Drawing. Murky.

"What did I draw for murky?" I ask. He nods.

"I wrote that word for a feeling," I say. "But a feeling isn't always drawable, so I drew the pond where I go swimming. There's a raft, and we dare each other to jump off and touch bottom. You have to go way down and the water gets ice cold, but the worse part is when you touch. The bottom's all squishy with old pine needles and mud that sucks your feet down, right to your ankles. By then you're almost out of air, and you start thinking maybe this time the mud won't let go and you won't make it back up. But the rule is that you have to bring back a handful of that murky stuff from the bottom to prove you made it all the way."

I expect disgust on Jason's face, but I see something else — wishing.

Is? Fun.

I nod. "Coming up makes it worth it."

He sighs and I realize he'll never feel the thrill of

breaking the surface, fist raised, mud dripping down his wrist. How can someone live a whole life and never feel that?

You. Said. You. Write. Murky. For. Feeling. Jason taps. What happened?

I reach down to finger the word cards beside me. "You know Kristi, my new neighbor I told you about? On Tuesday she came over. Which would've been great, except Ryan came with her. He's the boy I can't stand. David wanted some of Ryan's gum, but Ryan teased him and everything was —" Ruined.

"And the worst part," I whisper so Mom can't overhear, "David thinks Ryan's his *friend*. He doesn't understand Ryan's only making fun of him." I add the words fast. Cruel. Tease. Embarrassed. "And I get stuck making it better when it all goes wrong." Hate. Unfair.

Beside me, little yellow-white sand grains cling to the wheel of Jason's wheelchair. I wipe them away a few at a time and watch them disappear, too tiny to see fall.

"So I felt like that." I touch Murky. "Stuck at the bottom of the pond, only this time the mud wasn't letting go."

Sometimes. Jason hesitates, his fingers held in the air over his book. I. Wish. Die.

"Don't say that!"

Mrs. Morehouse startles. "What's wrong?"

I look from Jason's finger on Secret. to Mrs. Morehouse sitting forward in her chair. "He just surprised me, that's all." I flip through his pages to find words. I. Would. Miss. You.

Jason smiles.

But. Why? Wish. Die.

He shrugs. No. Word. Frustrating. Most.

I roll one last sand grain, perfect and sharp, between my finger and thumb.

I. Am. He turns the page in his book and points to Incomplete.

"No you're not. But I know what you mean. Sometimes I don't feel whole, either." I find an empty pocket for Torn. "I feel like I'm ripping in half. One half wanting to run away and be a regular person with my friends, but my other half is scared to leave David because he can't make it on his own."

Make. Word. Please.

I open my backpack and reach for a blank card. "What do you need?"

Leg. Go. Very much. Fast.

"Run?"

He nods and I scribble the letters, leaning forward, rushing across the top of the card.

Jason taps, Sometimes. Asleep. I. Dream. I. Can. Run.

"Really?"

He nods. How? Does. It. Feel. To. Run.

"Strong." I struggle for the right words. "And fast and in a weird way — weightless. Like if you could go fast enough, you'd fly. It's an amazing, free feeling." I squeeze my toes, imagining the slap of my sneakers on the sidewalk. "Is that how it feels in your dreams?"

No. He looks away from me, his lips pressed together.

How could I bring these words to comfort myself when they put that hurt in his face? "I could push you around the parking lot, really fast," I joke. "That'd be close to running."

Jason taps, Okay.

My smile freezes. "Okay?"

Sure. Why not?

Out the window, a man in a gray sweatshirt walks down the gift shop steps. A woman opens the door to Elliot's Antiques, and a family comes out of the restaurant, laughing. Between the rows of parked cars, a seagull struts, looking side to side.

"Because there are cars out there, and tourists," I say. "And seagulls!"

You. Can. Watch out!!! For. Car. Jason smiles. Bird. Will. Move.

"I don't think —"

Tell. Mom. I'll be right back. He stops his finger on Please.

I pull in a shaky breath. "Mrs. Morehouse? Jason and I are going out in the parking lot for a few minutes. We're going for a run." I say the last part extra quiet.

"A what?" She looks up from her magazine.

"A run." I step behind Jason's wheelchair and

push. It rolls smoothly, easier than I expected across the carpet.

"Do you really think this is a good idea?" Mrs. Morehouse asks as we pass her.

I can't see what Jason taps, but she moves to open the door. "Be careful, Catherine." She fixes me with a stern look.

I grip the wheelchair handles as we go down the ramp, my muscles tight as rope. My palms feel slick, but I don't dare relax even one finger, afraid he'll roll from me.

At the bottom of the ramp, we both let go a relieved sigh. I turn the wheelchair to face the parking lot. "If this gets too wild, lift your hand and I'll know to stop, okay?"

Jason nods. Run.

I jog, more a fast walk than a run. Jason's head and shoulders shake as I bump him over cracks in the tar. There's so much to watch out for: holes and rocks and sand near the side of the building.

I stop beside the Dumpster. "Sorry this is such a bouncy ride. Are you sure you want to do this?"

Run. Fast.

I start again, pushing Jason's chair ahead of me. I run past the fire hydrant and around the parking sign, keeping a lookout for cars pulling into or out of the parking lot. Every few feet I shoot a lightning-quick glance at Jason's hands.

He doesn't pick them up, just holds tightly to his communication book. So I make the first turn, running faster. Clouds of seagulls take to the air in front of us, quarreling and shrieking.

Running hard now, my feet pound the tar, the flap of seagull wings as loud as my breath in my ears. People are looking, but I try not to see them as real, just statues to run past.

At the final turn, I see Mrs. Morehouse standing in the entrance to the parking lot, her palm out like a traffic cop, keeping cars from pulling in.

I dash past the mailbox, the EXIT HERE sign, past Mrs. Morehouse.

Leaning into it, faster, harder, my feet slap the pavement, until it comes — that weightless, near-to-flying fastness. "Do you feel it?" I yell to the back of Jason's head.

But if he answers, it's only in his head.

I run all the way to the clinic ramp. "How was that?"

Awesome!

I bend over to steady my breath. When I straighten up, I see not only is everyone in the waiting room standing at the clinic windows watching us, but a family on the sidewalk is staring, shopping bags in hand. And in several of the restaurant windows surrounding the parking lot, people have stopped eating to watch. Most of them have their mouths dropped open.

Jason waves.

A man in one of the restaurants gives a thumbs-up, and everyone in the waiting room cheers, Carol holding her baby high so he can see.

"One more time?" I ask Jason.

He grins. Excellent!

And we're off! Past the windows and the Dumpster, around the parking sign. Seagulls billowing into the air at every turn.

Strong, flying-fast, and free, we run.

Sometimes people don't answer because they didn't hear you. Other times it's because they don't *want* to hear you.

Though my legs are tired, I run faster up my driveway, trying to put every feeling into words for Jason's cards. Fierce, hard — my sneakers slap the tar — swift, brisk. I take off across the lawn (squishy, springy), but as I round the far corner of the house, my feet slow to a walk.

Dad is kneeling in our garden, his back to me. Watching him, I think of Kristi at her dad's for the weekend and Melissa in California with hers. Part of me wants to run up and hug Dad from behind or cover his eyes with my hands, like I did when I was little. "Guess who?" I'd say and he'd guess everyone but me — even though we both knew he was pretending because he'd give impossible answers like "Queen Elizabeth" or "Little Bo Peep."

Before I can decide what to do, Dad spots me.

"Look, Cath." He twists a ripe tomato from the vine and holds it out to me. "Isn't this beautiful? I'm sure not many people have ripe tomatoes yet."

I walk over and take it from him. "I bet we're the first."

Dad's always proud we have tomatoes before anyone else. That's because he starts the seeds in pots on the kitchen windowsill while snow's still deep on the ground.

I study the tomato closely, drawing it in my mind. It's so smooth I'd need dense color, layered until not even a flicker of white paper showed through. Alone, each of my colored pencils would be too bright, but blended, I could make it look real. "People usually think tomatoes are red," I say, "but they're more red-orange with yellow-orange streaks. And there's even the smallest hint of purple here in the creases."

"Purple?" He looks over, his forehead lined with concern. "Is it mold?"

It feels stupid to be jealous of a tomato, but sometimes I think Dad likes them more than he likes David and me. "No, it's just a shadow."

"Oh, good." Dad turns a frilly leaf to check the underside. Standing above him, I'm startled to see more gray hair than brown on the top of Dad's head. When did that happen?

"Have you heard from Melissa lately?" he asks.

"I got a postcard last week. Her father took her to Disneyland." I roll my tomato between my hands, the prickly stem poking into my palm. "Maybe you and I could do something special, too? Just us?"

He sighs like it's the millionth thing I've asked him for today, instead of the first. "You know we can't afford something like that."

"I don't mean Disneyland. Just something, me and you."

Dad smiles, but it's a worn-out smile that doesn't light his eyes. "I'm sorry, honey. I've been dealing with doctors and customers and staff all week. I really need to stay home today and be quiet a while."

Watching him pick another tomato, I mouth words at the back of his head: "But what about me?"

"Maybe we could cook spaghetti tonight?" He places his tomato with the others in his basket. "These would make a great sauce."

Before I can answer, Mom yells, "It's three o'clock."

Dad frowns at his watch. "I'd really like to finish up here first," he calls to her. "I'm almost done."

In the kitchen doorway, Mom crosses her arms over her stomach. "David has his shoes on already, and I have paperwork to do for my meeting on Monday."

"I'll be there in a minute," Dad shouts.

The sound of Mom slamming the kitchen door makes me cringe. I'm torn between wanting to yell at him for choosing tomatoes over Mom and wanting to cry that he's choosing David over me. "Maybe we could go to the mall?"

"You heard Mom, I have to take David to the video store. Do you want to come with us?"

"No, thanks. Maybe we could do something afterward?"

"Someday soon," he says. "I promise."

I drop my tomato in his basket with the others. I know he's just promising to stop me from asking again. Walking away I turn once to check if Dad's watching me go. *Look for me.* Staring at the back of his head, I imagine him turning left and right, searching.

He picks another tomato.

No toys in the fish tank.

Monday morning my heart jumps to see the minivan in the driveway next door when I wake up. I get dressed and eat my breakfast in little bites so if Kristi calls I won't answer with a mouthful of cereal.

At nine o'clock the phone rings. "I'll get it!" I yell in the direction of the kitchen where Mom and David are still having breakfast.

Please don't let it be one of Mom's clients. Or Dad calling from work. I wait two more rings so it won't seem like I was waiting next to the phone. "Hello?"

"Hi, Catherine? It's Kristi."

I mouth "yes!" to keep from squealing. "Hi."

"I was wondering if you want to do something? I don't have to be at the community center until noon."

"Sure. That'd be great."

"Could we hang out at your house? Mine is crazy today," Kristi says. "Mom forgot to tell me the plumber was coming, and now I can't even have a shower."

I'd like to say, "You can shower at my house" to be nice, but with David home, the embarrassment chances are too risky. "Want to go swimming?"

"There's a pool?"

"It's a pond, but it's not far. There's a raft and a little beach that anyone can use."

She hesitates so long, I ask, "Are you still there?"

"I'll be over in a few minutes."

In my bedroom I tug open the top drawer of my bureau to pick a bathing suit. The blue one-piece is good for swimming but not pretty. I love the purple-and-white bikini that looks like batik, but the top slides when I dive. So I'm left with the last suit: green with gold flowers, swimmable and not ugly.

Though I'm hurrying, I take a couple of seconds to stroke on cherry lip gloss and pink eye shadow, and comb my hair. Maybe I'll try my hair loose today, parted a little on the side.

With jean shorts over my bathing suit, my favorite beach towel draped around my neck, sunscreen lathered, and flip-flops on, I'm ready.

Mom's still in the kitchen with David. Kneeling beside a pile of wet paper towels, she's cleaning a milk puddle from the linoleum. At the table David swings his legs, eating his cereal.

"Kristi and I are going to the pond," I say. "I'll be back by lunch."

Mom looks up from the spilled milk. "I'm heading to the store. Would you like me to drop you girls off on the way?"

"No, thanks. We'll walk."

She gathers the wet paper towels. "David, when you're finished, get your shoes on. We need to go to the grocery store and buy something for lunch."

He looks up from his bowl of cereal at the table, milk drops clinging to his chin. "And a video?"

"Okay, but just this time."

David bolts from his seat, pushing past me to drop his bowl in the sink. "Watch out, Frog!" he cries, bits of cereal splashing on the counter.

"Say 'Excuse me, *Catherine*.'" When he doesn't say it, Mom gets up to block the doorway. "Excuse me, *Catherine*," she repeats, looking over her glasses at David.

The doorbell rings.

"See you later!" I squeeze past David and under Mom's arm. Though my name's part of the conversation, it's got nothing to do with me.

I race down the hallway to the front door, but as soon as I see Kristi, I wish I'd picked the purple-and-white bikini. She looks pretty in a long T-shirt and sandals, her hair hanging over her shoulder in a single braid. "Can I borrow a beach towel?" she asks. "I couldn't find mine."

"Sure, I'll go grab one."

When I come back to the living room with my second-favorite beach towel, Kristi giggles. "There's a *duck* in your fish tank."

Behind her, the aquarium cover juts out at a crooked angle. In the tank David's rubber duck bobs along the surface, a goldfish mouthing his tail.

"Come on." I fake a smile, handing her the towel. "Let's go."

Outside the air smells summery, of mown grass and warm tar, and from somewhere high in the trees I hear a woodpecker rapping.

David is gone with Mom and I'm free, walking down the road with Kristi.

"I've never been swimming in a pond," Kristi says, "only in pools and the ocean."

"It's fun." I make sure to keep in step with Kristi. "Much warmer than the ocean — at least in Maine. It's gooey at the bottom when you're out a ways, but that's only old pine needles and leaves. Once you get in, you probably won't notice a big difference from a pool."

She doesn't look so sure.

Approaching the corner, I can't believe how ordinary the bus stop looks in the summer, only another bend of sidewalk. Kristi slows, staring at Ryan's empty yard.

Was I her second choice?

. . .

"Are there fish in here?" Kristi asks, kicking her sandals off on the sand.

I follow her gaze out across the pond to the fringe of pine and white birch trees on the other shore. "Only minnows come near the shore."

On our side of the pond there's a strip of sandy beach, but the far side has a steep, scooped-out bank, tangled with bushes and the roots of trees. "Once I overheard Ryan tell someone that there's a big fish that lives under the raft," I say, still smarting from Kristi's long look at his house. "But I've never seen it, so he might be lying."

Kristi wraps her fingers around her braid. "Is it deep?"

"Over my head, but not so deep I can't swim down and touch. Sometimes we dare each other to bring back muck from the bottom."

Her knuckles whiten on her braid.

"But *we* don't have to do that," I say.

"Good." She walks to the shore, pulling off her

T-shirt. Seeing her candy-red bikini, I wish again I'd worn my purple-and-white one, even if I had to hold the top when I dove.

I undo my shorts. "I like your bathing suit."

"I wanted to wear the new one my aunt gave me. But I think it's with my laundry at Dad's." Kristi points her foot, skimming the water with her toes.

Standing in the pond, my ankles look crooked, cut by the water's surface. I study the waterline's ripple of distortion, wanting to capture it in my sketchbook.

"That's a bad part of living in two places." Kristi shudders, stepping into the pond with me. "I never have what I need at the right house. And Mom doesn't get it. This morning she kept saying, 'Just wear another bathing suit.' like it didn't matter."

Watching her adjust the straps of her bikini top, I want to tell her I know how it feels to be split down the middle, too. Pulled between the regular world of school and friends, and David's world where none of the same things matter. And how I don't belong completely in either world, but —

When someone is upset, it's not a good time to bring up your own problems.

Kristi takes a step farther into the water. "I hate this bathing suit. The straps are always falling down."

I'm in water to my knees now. "I know what you mean. The top of my favorite bikini doesn't fit perfect, and it slides. It's never *shown* anything, but . . ."

Kristi smiles. "I had a bathing suit like that once. It drove me crazy."

Stepping deeper, the cold tingles my thighs. I rub the goose bumps on my arms. "It's always chilly at first, but you'll get used to it. I promise."

"Catherine, I'm sorry about the other day with the gum."

I turn, but she's not looking at me. Chin down, Kristi skims her fingertips across the surface of the water.

"David doesn't get jokes sometimes." The water feels warmer on my legs and I take another step.

"Ryan didn't mean to upset him. He told me so."

He didn't mean to upset *you*. The tiny waves created

from Kristi's hands moving the water make a freezing tickle on my stomach.

"He said —"

"The bottom gets gooey here," I say to change the subject. "If you dive in now, you don't have to feel it." Plunging forward, my chest and shoulders scream with the shock of cold. I go under, breaststroking, kicking hard, until my lungs ache and I can't stay under one second more.

Breaking the surface, my hair is plastered to my face. I tread water, pushing it away.

Kristi stands in the shallows, her hands tracing across the pond's surface.

"Come on," I say. "It's not bad once you get in."

She takes a step. "Are you kidding? It's freezing."

"Not once you get used to it. I'll meet you at the raft."

I love swimming in water over my head, cold emptiness under my feet, those sudden warm spots or icy underwater springs.

Almost to the raft, I flip to my back and give in to the lightness of floating. Held by the water, I watch the blue sky, waiting for Kristi to catch up. This is what I wished for — a next-door friend I could just come and go with.

She's out of breath when she reaches me.

At the ladder I grip the sides and swing my feet up to the bottom rung. Water showers off me as I climb.

"About that big fish?" Kristi says, swimming closer. "What kind is it?"

The air makes me shiver. I sit on the raft and wrap my arms around my knees. "It's probably just an eel."

Her eyes widen.

"I mean it's probably *not* an eel. Just a fish that *looks* like an eel."

Kristi scrambles up the ladder. "Yuck!"

I tuck my soaked hair behind my ears, wishing I had brought my hair band. I know without asking, Kristi won't want to touch the bottom. She doesn't even seem to like the *top* of the water much. "Maybe we can lay out in the sun?"

We lie on our stomachs, and I peek between the slats to the darkness below. The slight rocking of the raft, the slosh of little waves slapping the boards beneath, and the sun drying my back makes me yawn.

"I have to find my other suit."

I look over to Kristi fixing her shoulder straps.

"But if it's not at Dad's, I don't know where it is." She lays her chin on her arm. "I wish Mom wouldn't give up so easy. It's not like he had an affair."

"Maybe they're just taking a break for a little while?"

"Maybe." Kristi sighs. "Do you think there really is a fish down there?"

The sadness in her voice makes me want to give her something, even if it's only pretend. "What if he *is* down there," I say, "but he's magic like in that fairy tale 'The Fisherman and His Wife.'"

Kristi squeezes the end of her braid, drops of water falling off the tip, beading onto the raft. "I don't know that story."

"This guy catches a big fish, except the fish says he is really a prince under a spell. The man lets the fish go, but his wife sends him back to get a wish granted."

"I'd scream if a fish started talking to me."

"Me, too. But what would you wish?"

"I'd wish my parents would get back together and be happy." She turns to me, her eyes worried. "Do you think that's two wishes or one?"

"One."

"Your turn. What's your wish?"

I look down between the raft boards and imagine my always-wish, my fingers reaching through the perfect top of David's head, finding the broken places in his brain, turning knobs or flipping switches. All his autism wiped clean.

But saying that wish brings trouble. "All people have a place," my third-grade teacher said firmly when I drew a pretend older brother in the "My Family" picture to be put out in the hallway for open house.

I tried to tell her it was still David — but I wanted him to be able to play with me, and since I was fixing things, I made him older so he could stick up for *me*. But I had to draw the picture over and visit the guidance counselor instead of going to music.

"Why is it in fairy tales, wishes always backfire?" I ask.

If you want to change the subject, confuse the other person by going off on a wild, chatty detour.

"Like in 'The Fisherman and His Wife,'" I continue. "The fisherman's wife keeps wanting bigger things, and by the end of the story —"

"Hey!" a voice calls. "Kris!"

I sit up so quick, I scrape my knees on the raft.

Ryan waves, standing on the sand at the shore. Behind him his bike rests propped against a tree.

Kristi waves back. "Hi!"

I hope she yells at him to go home, but she says, "Come on, Catherine," and does a running dive, heading for shore.

I let her swim ahead of me. I do the breaststroke, dipping my face in and out of the water, so I don't have to see Ryan standing on the sand waiting for us.

At the shore I cross my arms over my stomach and walk to my shorts and towel.

"Your mom said you were here," Ryan says to Kristi. "Did you ask Catherine yet?"

Ask me?

Kristi smiles. "Catherine, you know how the community center's holding a dance on Saturday?"

I nod.

"They asked me to help decorate," Kristi says, "and I was hoping —"

"I could help you decorate," I say, grabbing my towel off the sand. "I'm good at making posters."

"Actually, I was hoping you'd like to go?" Kristi glances at Ryan. "Me and Ryan and you and somebody. It'll be so much fun. Please say yes."

I wrap my towel around me, tight as I can. "I don't know anyone to ask."

"Ask Jason," Kristi says. "That boy you drew. This is your chance to ask him out."

I open my mouth, but Ryan's smirk makes me close it.

But that's not the only reason I don't tell.

"I don't dance." I slide my feet into my flip-flops.

"I'll teach you," Kristi says.

"My dad works late a lot so I don't think I could get a ride."

"My mom can drop us off and pick us up."

On the walk home, Kristi has an answer for every one of my can'ts. She'll even loan me clothes and do my hair.

"Ask him," she says.

By the time she's heading up her driveway, Kristi has cornered me into a stuttered, "Hmm. I'll think about it."

In my room I peel off my damp bathing suit and put on the first clothes I pull from my bureau, an old shirt and shorts that don't match.

I comb wet snarls from my hair and watch Kristi's minivan backing out of their driveway. Did Kristi call me because she can't go to the dance with Ryan unless I go, too?

The minivan disappears from view. I turn to my bulletin board and the postcard from Disneyland tacked on the top. I wish it wasn't so expensive to call California. I want to tell Melissa everything and hear her say, "It's okay, Catherine." But it'd take too long to explain and maybe she'd be mad I cared so much about Kristi being my friend.

In my sketchbook I try to draw my ankles distorted by pond water, but they don't look warped and interesting. They look broken.

I write words in the white space beside the sketch, but after 'pond' and 'icy' the only ones that'll come are: 'guilty,' 'complicated,' 'hidden,' and 'weak.'

I close my sketchbook.

Solving one problem can create another.

I look over the top of my sketchbook at Jason's mother standing alone.

Before I can ask where Jason is, she opens the door and he comes into the waiting room — on his own!

He has a new wheelchair with a joystick on the armrest. His fingers circle the joystick, and the wheelchair whirrs past the front windows, across the carpet, right up beside me.

"Wow!" I toss my sketchbook on the waiting room couch.

"How wonderful!" Mom says.

"He never wanted a motorized chair before." Mrs. Morehouse smiles at Mom. "But lately he wants to do *lots* of things for himself. He's even doing his hand exercises again."

Jason reddens, flipping open his communication book.

"And since his birthday is this weekend," Mrs. Morehouse continues, "his father and I knew this would be the perfect present for him."

"This is cool." I lean close for a good look. "How's it work?"

Jason positions his hand on the joystick, and the chair surges — a foot forward, then back. Catherine. Walk. Outside. Me, too.

"You want to take a walk? Outside?" I glance at his mother. "With *me*?"

"Take my cell phone." She opens her purse. "Call here if you need help. The phone number is on those business cards at the reception desk."

The receptionist circles the phone number on the card. But even with the number, the cell phone, two blank cards, and a pencil in my pocket, I don't feel prepared. What if I can't help him? Or he needs something, and I can't understand him?

I hold the door open and on his fourth try, Jason makes the turn around the door frame. All the way down the ramp, I hold my breath, repeating *slow, slow* in my head like a prayer, so he doesn't go too fast and tip or fall.

At the bottom of the ramp, I let my breath go in a relieved *whoosh*. "Where to?"

Clusters of people stand near the shops and the brick sidewalks look too bumpy and uneven for a wheelchair. I wish I could take Jason to Elliot's Antiques and show him all the bottles and old things, but there is a long flight of stairs, and the aisles are too narrow for a wheelchair.

Water. Jason taps.

"You need a drink?"

Go. To. Water.

Between the buildings, waves glitter with sun diamonds. I scan the route for problems: down the parking lot (watch out for broken tar and the sewer grate), cross the street (easy), go to the driveway at Otis's Hardware and use the little ramp to the curb (a sharp turn), down the sidewalk in front of Coastal

Marine Supply (looks good from here). After that, smooth paths run all the way through the waterfront park (home free). I glance back to the clinic. Mom and Mrs. Morehouse wave from the window. "Okay, but we can't stay long. Your mom will be mad if you miss speech."

Whatever. Speech.

I walk beside his wheelchair and imitate Speech Woman, "WELL, JASON! I GUESS YOUR DAY STINKS A —"

Footsteps pound behind us, and two women jog by, one on each side of Jason and me. One of the women gives Jason a soft-eyed pity look.

Watching the soles of their sneakers running away, I push my hands into my pockets, touching my pencil, the business card, and the flat-topped buttons of Jason's mother's cell phone.

Maybe I shouldn't have agreed to go so far.

As we reach the crosswalk, a car stops for us. I stare at the curls of hair on the back of Jason's neck as we cross the street.

An old couple stands at the curb, the woman

hunting for something in her purse. "Excuse me," I say. "We need the ramp."

"Oh, sorry!" The man glances at Jason's legs. They move on, the woman still searching her purse.

I walk ahead on the sidewalk, kicking away pinecones and rocks and sticks so his chair won't get stuck on them. When I turn back, Jason's coming up behind me, his fingers resting in sharp angles on his communication book, his eyes fixed on the water.

"It's beautiful, isn't it?" I say.

He nods. More than. Awesome! What?

"What word means more than awesome?"

Yes.

Looking across the sun-dazzled waves, I have no word. "I think after 'awesome,' you're done with words."

Make. Card. More than. Words.

Even though we're blocking the sidewalk and people have to step on the grass to go around us, I take a blank card from my pocket and write 'more than words' across the top. Searching for something to draw, not even the ocean seems enough.

No. Picture.

In his book the card stands out against the others I've made, plain as a field of new snow. "You're right," I say. "This way it can be anything you imagine."

The air smells fishy, a green-brown, deep-water smell. I choose the path winding along the shore, leading to a row of red-painted benches facing the ocean.

Down the shoreline a fishing boat pulls up to the dock at the seafood restaurant, and a man in a long white apron rushes down the gangplank to meet the boat.

Side by side, Jason and I take up the whole path. A girl bumps my arm rushing around us, walking two black poodles.

"Sorry," she says over her shoulder.

I whisper to Jason, "She's late for the dog show."

Jason flashes me a grin.

"Maybe that bench by the wharf?" Usually I love listening to the pilings creaking, purring boat motors, and the sharp *key-ow* of gulls, but today my ears are full of the sound of Jason's wheelchair and the silence of people who suddenly stop talking as we pass.

A man meets my gaze. He smiles but I can only nod back, unable to let go the clench of my teeth.

At the long town wharf, a seagull stands on twig legs, facing the wind, shaking his feathers dry. He reaches around to preen his wing as a group of preschoolers leans over the wharf railing, dropping rocks off the side.

I hear snatches of voices as we come closer to the wharf.

"You don't even need this, but it'll make you feel better." Reaching down, a girl puts a bandage on a little boy's elbow.

Her head is bowed but I know her hair, parted on the side, a strand separate from having been twirled. I fall to one knee on the path and dip my head to peer between the slats of an empty bench.

"Was that boy in an accident?" the child says, pointing at Jason. "Did he get hurt?"

I watch Kristi startle, looking at Jason. She turns away quickly and touches her index finger to the child's lips. "Shh. It's not polite to talk about people."

Jason backs his wheelchair up the path toward me,

and I lean so his chair is between Kristi and me. He stops, struggling to look over his shoulder at me. "I'm coming," I say.

He taps, but I can't see his communication book from the ground and I'm too scared to stand up. My shoelace is tied but I hold the loops in my fingers, knowing when I let go, I'll have to do something. Why can't I just stand up and say, "Hi, Kristi?"

"Okay, grab your partner's hand, everyone," a woman yells. "Time to get back to the bus."

I peek, enough to see Kristi take the child's hand. She follows the line of children, stuffing bandage wrappers in her shorts pocket.

I stand slowly. "I'm all set."

At the empty bench closest to the wharf, I sit on the very edge of the wooden seat and watch Kristi growing tinier the farther she walks down the pathway.

Jason taps, and I tear my focus away from Kristi passing the last streetlight at the edge of the park. Catherine. Pretty. Today.

I nod. "It's a very pretty day."

Jason touches my arm. Catherine. Pretty.

My neck feels prickly. I rub it, looking down to a frill of seaweed, bits of rope, and a broken lobster trap caught between the huge rocks at the water's edge. What does he mean? Is he being nice or telling me he *likes* me?

When things get confusing, make a joke.

"No." I cross my eyes at him. "I'm a dork."

Jason doesn't smile.

"We should get back. Speech Woman will be coming out to get you." But Jason doesn't circle his fingers on the joystick. He turns to a new page in his communication book. My birthday party. Do you want to come?

The cards sit alone on the page, new and homemade. My birthday party. has red and blue balloons and a chocolate-brown cake.

I don't know why, but I feel jealous that his mom made him nicer cards than usual. But that feeling mixes with sadness that he had to ask her to make these words so he could invite me to his party.

I tell myself it's a simple invitation to a birthday party, not a date. "Sure. When's your party?"

Saturday.

My breath catches. "*This* Saturday?"

Jason nods. Is? Good.

"Yeah, it's great! No problem at all."

Walking back to the clinic, a woman reading on the grass stares over the top of her book at Jason. I stare back.

Even though I told Jason it was great that his party is Saturday, it's more than great — it solves everything.

Almost.

No dancing unless I'm alone in my room or it's pitch-black dark.

"Six!" David calls as a gray pickup drives by on the road. "And thirty-six minutes twenty-seven seconds."

I wish I could just walk up Kristi's porch steps and ring the doorbell like nothing happened today at the park. But I can't get my feet to move.

"Seven cars." David holds out his watch. "And thirty-five minutes fifty-five seconds."

"Remember the rule," I say absently. "Late doesn't mean not coming."

Beside me on the porch swing, David rocks, bobbling the swing. When I first agreed to sit with David so Mom could call clients, I tried to draw, but David keeps jogging the swing out of rhythm, wobbling my pencil lines.

What'll happen in September? Will Kristi stand with me at the bus stop or with Ryan? And what'll happen when I don't see Jason every week? Will our friendship disappear?

The front door opens and Mom steps onto our porch. "Catherine, Kristi's on the phone. David, let's go in the backyard."

The walk through the living room and down the hallway to the phone feels extra long. Did Kristi see me at the park?

"Hi, it's Kristi," she says when I pick up the phone. "I just got home from the day camp, and I signed up to make two posters to use at the dance. Want to help?"

"Sure." I twist the phone cord around my finger. "Um, about the dance —"

"Did you ask Jason?"

I twist the cord tighter, my fingertip turning purple with backed-up blood. "We can't come to the dance. Jason invited me to his birthday party that same day."

"His birthday party?"

"Yeah, he's having a birthday party on Saturday."

"How about after the party?"

"I really can't," I say, my finger throbbing.

Kristi exhales loud and long in my ear. "Will you still help me make posters? I promised to make two big ones."

"Sure." I untwist the phone cord.

"Let's make them at your house. Mom's taking a nap."

I check out the window for David. He's swinging hard on the wooden swing set Dad made him. Mom rests against the slide, her cell phone to her ear.

Leaning way back, David laughs, his eyes scrunched shut as he pumps his legs. I can't stand that feeling — free-falling through the sky with my eyes closed — but David loves it.

"Come on over."

In my room I collect markers, pencils, my ruler, paints, and brushes, until Kristi arrives.

Her blank, white poster board reminds me of Jason's cards, only huge.

"We need one sign for the admission desk and one for the refreshment stand." Kristi lays the poster board on my checkered rug. "Which one do you want to make?"

I shrug. "I'll make the one for the admission desk."

"It needs to say 'dance' and how much it costs," Kristi says.

Kneeling in front of the poster board, there's so much whiteness, I'm tempted to find a soft-lead pencil and draw tiny footprints, maybe two sets, walking through a windswept field of snow.

My marker squeaks as I write each huge red letter: D tipping forward, A leaning back, N shivery, C stretched tall, and the lines of E poking out at funny angles, the word itself dancing. I begin a border of fireworks exploding around the edges of the poster. Awesome fireworks.

"You're a good artist," Kristi says, grimacing at her pillow-fat letters spelling "Refreshments." R is big, but each letter after is a little smaller, like if the word kept going and going, it'd disappear.

"Maybe if you color them in?"

She picks up a yellow marker.

"I think I need another color on these fireworks." I show her my poster. "What do you think?"

"You didn't use green." Kristi hands me the marker. "I still wish you were coming to the dance."

"It's better since I don't dance — in fact, I have a rule against it. No dancing unless I'm alone in my room or it's pitch-black dark."

Kristi huffs. "That's a dumb —"

My door bangs open. For a change I'm glad to see David standing there, his face flushed from swinging.

"David, do you like to dance?" Kristi stands up.

Holding the green marker, I look between David waiting in my doorway and Kristi choosing a CD from my shelf. "Let's show Catherine how."

"Don't." I scramble to my feet. "He'll step on the posters."

But Kristi starts my Avril Lavigne CD. "Come on, David." She shimmies her body, elbows bent, her hair swinging. "Let's dance."

When David dances, it's from his heart, from the inside out. Jumping around my room in an all-over wiggly dance, feet kicking, he steps on markers. Cinnamon and Nutmeg start squealing.

"Quiet, pigs!" David claps his hands over his ears.

"Stop it!" I snatch the posters off the floor as his heel snaps my ruler in half. Stumbling across the room to my CD player, I wince as markers jab my bare feet.

I turn the music off.

"Why'd you do that?" Kristi asks.

As I lay the posters back on the floor, I hear a car door slam outside.

David is gone from my room so fast my calendar flutters in the breeze he makes running past.

"Ready to go, sport?" I hear Dad call — late again.

"You're no fun." Kristi flops back onto my rug.

Behind my eyes, I feel the sizzle of tears. I want to be fun, but — "I don't like when people make David look stupid."

"I asked him to dance. How is that making him look stupid? He liked it, didn't he?" Her marker squeaks, scribbling hard strokes.

Kneeling beside her, I uncap the green marker. "Did your mom say you can only go to the dance with Ryan if I go, too?"

"I thought you said you *couldn't* go."

"I can't."

"Then it doesn't matter," she says, not looking at me.

We finish our posters, barely talking. Green ruins my fireworks. I trace the lines and bursts, wishing there were a way to go backward and make them what I wanted them to be.

Not everything worth keeping has to be useful.

I open the door that says ELLIOT'S ANTIQUES, tucked between the two storefronts, and climb the wide staircase.

I love this place: the jumble of old, glittery broaches in the glass case, the worn pots and dishes and frayed baskets on the bookshelves. I can't help stopping at the display of old bottles. If I had lots of money, I'd buy that ruby one for my bedroom windowsill. With sunlight shining through, I bet it's beautiful.

"Can I help you?" Elliot stands up, behind his desk. His desktop is buried with piles of papers and used books.

Elliot is thin and old and always stooped, like he

got tired of having to duck his head, so he does it always now.

"I'm looking for a guitar."

I knew I couldn't afford a new one at a department store or music store, and I don't know if I can even afford an Elliot guitar, but I have to find out.

He steps away from his desk and over boxes to reach me in the aisle. "I have a couple." He adjusts his glasses on his sharp nose.

I follow him through the maze of old chairs and tables covered with tools to the instruments. There's a saxophone in an open case, looking dull against the black velvet. An organ is pushed against the wall, and next to that are three snare drums stacked one on top of the other. Four guitars rest against the side of the drums.

Elliot shows them to me, and I can *almost* afford the cheapest acoustic one. It's scratched and dusty, which is good news for me.

Most places the price is the price, but sometimes Elliot will "take an offer," especially if it's something he's had a long time and would like to get rid of. I show him my money.

"That's all I have."

"All right," he says, and I own a guitar.

Carrying it down the stairs, I worry that Jason will see me in the parking lot with the guitar, so I race to our car and quickly put it in the backseat.

In the waiting room, I take out the words I made: Seagull. Wharf. Park. Sailboat. Pathway. Bench. Together. I made these cards extra special, the pictures detailed and beautiful. I want to remember the good parts of our walk, not the part with me on the ground, hiding from Kristi, hoping Jason won't notice.

When they arrive, Mrs. Morehouse looks to Jason's finger stabbing his communication book. "Don't 'whatever' me, young man!"

Jason whirrs up beside me. Hi. Catherine. Time. 1:00. My birthday party.

"Great! I'll be there." I reach toward an empty pocket in his communication book with Seagull. but Jason grabs my arm to stop me. Your. Brother. Can. Come.

"To your party?" David would love to go, but it'll be harder for me if he does. "I don't know if that's a good idea. He'll want to watch your TV, and he'll need to know if your cellar door's closed, and —"

OK. With. Me.

Jason looks like he means it, so I suggest, "Maybe he could come at the end and have a piece of cake?"

Jason nods. Your. Neighbor. Friend. Can. Come. Too.

"I'm sure Kristi's busy with Ryan on Saturday, but thanks for inviting her." I show him my cards. "Look, I made you words from the park."

Awesome! He smiles. Mom. Bought. New. Book. For. More. Words.

I put Seagull. in a pocket. "That's good, because you're almost out of room in this one."

In fact, by the time I'm done, Together. has to go on the final page of his communication book. It sits by itself, a picture of the bench with two people sitting on it.

Where? Wheelchair. Jason pulls his brows together.

"I imagined you without it. Like in your dream where you can run."

Want. Wheelchair. In. Picture.

"I just thought —"

Take. It. Out. Jason looks away, frowning.

I remove the card. "I remembered your dream. I thought you might like that."

"Is everything all right?" Mrs. Morehouse asks. I look over to see her staring at us. "Jason?" she asks. "Do you need something?"

He puts his hand over the wheelchair joystick and whirrs through the waiting room, down the corridor.

"I don't think Jennifer's ready for you," Mrs. Morehouse calls. "She usually comes out to get you."

I feel everyone looking at me. I slide Together. under my leg to hide it.

"Catherine?" Mom asks. "What happened?"

Ignoring Mom, I pick up my sketchbook and turn to my rule collection.

But I don't know what to write.

Pantless brothers are not my problem.

On Saturday Mom parks our car in front of a sprawling modern house with tall windows and a long wooden ramp leading to the front door.

I'm not sure I can do this. I glance to the rearview mirror and see Mom's eyes looking at me.

"Save a piece of cake?" David flickers his fingers beside me in the car.

"At four o'clock." I catch his hand and hold it still so he'll pay attention. "Here are your rules." I pass him a sheet of paper.

David reads aloud, "'Chew with your mouth closed. Don't open or close doors at other people's houses. Don't look in their refrigerator or turn on their TV. Use a fork for cake, not your fingers.'"

"Catherine, I'll watch him," Mom says. "Don't worry."

Getting out of the car, I'm tempted to yell, "Oh, yeah? Like you watched him at Melissa's?" but I have bigger worries.

Walking to the ramp, I clutch the bag of fancy jelly beans, the birthday card I painted with watercolors of guinea pigs eating cake ("Pig Out on Your Birthday!"), and the guitar wrapped in two white plastic trash bags, a huge red bow tied around the neck. It was the best wrapping I could come up with for something so big.

My pulse beats with my footsteps on the ramp, and as I get closer to Jason's front door, I hear a thumping bass line and muted laughter.

I stab the doorbell. Part of me wants to drop the guitar on the welcome mat and jump into the shrubs, but before I can move, the door opens.

I look up at a teenaged boy with familiar wavy reddish-brown hair. "Hi," he says. "I'm Matt, Jason's brother."

"I'm Catherine."

"Oh, you're Catherine?" He grins, raising one eyebrow. "You've made Jason some cool cards."

I blush. Of course, everyone who talks to Jason sees my cards. Why didn't I ever think of that?

"Come in. I'll tell Jason you're here."

The living room is crowded with people. Some adults and kids sit in chairs spread around the room, talking and laughing. Others stand at the table drinking coffee and soda. On the couch there's a family with two little kids. The mother smiles at me and I smile back.

But I don't see Jason anywhere. I hold the guitar at my side so it's less noticeable.

"Catherine!" Mrs. Morehouse comes toward me. "Welcome. There's pizza in the kitchen. Grab a plate and make yourself at home. Matt, we could use a few more chairs. Would you get the ones off the back porch?"

She's wearing a skirt and heels, and I kick myself for not putting on lip gloss or wearing something nicer than jean shorts and a T-shirt. When she steps close, I say, "Did you know Jason invited my brother to come for a piece of cake?"

"Yes. I'll put a big piece aside for David."

Glancing at the people talking and laughing loudly, and all those doorknobs David'll want to turn, I worry coming was a mistake.

I add the card and jelly beans to the presents piled on the table and sit next to an older woman, sliding the guitar under my chair. I should've brought Jason a music CD. I swallow, imagining him opening a beat-up guitar in front of all these people.

"Hello," the woman says, her hands smoothing the lap of her cotton dress. "Isn't this a lovely party?"

"Yes," I say. "Do you know where —?"

"Jason." Mrs. Morehouse calls. "There you are. Catherine's here."

In the doorway to the kitchen, Jason turns his head until he sees me. I walk over, wishing he'd smile or frown or anything that'd tell me if he's still mad. But Jason's mouth stays a flat line.

"Happy birthday," I say. "I left something on the present table for you, but I have another present, too."

Thank you.

I tap, Secret. Jason moves his hands away so I can turn the pages of his communication book.

I tap, I want. Open. Present. I reach into my shorts pocket and pull out Together.

On the card I drew myself sitting on the red bench and Jason beside me in his wheelchair.

"I'm sorry."

Jason smiles. Me, too. Come. With. Me. He gestures to the hallway, and I slide the guitar out from under the chair. Following him, I hold the guitar behind my back, counting four doors for David to open before Jason goes through a doorway.

A shiver passes between my shoulder blades. Though there's a houseful of people down the hall, it feels sneaky and wrong to step into a boy's bedroom.

On the wall over Jason's bed, between two baseball posters, is my drawing of Kristi's house.

And in front of the window is an electric piano.

"Is that your piano?" I ask.

He nods and turns the page in his communication book. I. Play. Bad. But. Like. It.

"I'd love to hear you play." I bring the guitar out from behind my back. "Sorry about the wrapping, but I couldn't really disguise it."

I untie the bow, and he pulls away the trash-bag wrapping. Nobody'd mistake the guitar for new, but I cleaned it until it shone.

"Mom took it to the music store and they put new strings on and tuned it," I say. "That part's a present from David, but the guitar's from me."

He smiles wide. Thank you. Catherine. Perfect. Guitar.

"You're welcome." I lay it across his wheelchair and he traces his fingers across the strings. It sounds rich and mysterious, lingering in the air even after his hand moves away.

Dazzling! He gestures for me to put his guitar on his bed.

I take the guitar from him and set it on his pillow. Behind me, I hear Jason cross the room to the window.

Music startles me. I spin to see Jason's shoulders bowed forward, his hands reaching over his wheelchair tray to the keyboard. I walk over to look closer at his fingers. Bent nearly double, his fingers touch the keys much like he touches his cards, one at a time. It's a simple song, spare and haunting.

"That's beautiful."

My. Own. Music.

"Jason?" a voice calls.

I turn. His mother stands in the doorway, smiling. "Grandpa needs to leave soon, so let's do your cake now."

Jason backs up and turns for the hallway. I sweep a last look across the piano, the guitar left on his pillow, the baseball posters, and my drawing of Kristi's house.

Walking down the hallway, I hear people singing "Happy Birthday," but I hum Jason's song under their singing. I want to remember it.

The cake is chocolate, my favorite, but I move the cake bits around on my plate, squeezing them flat with my fork.

Beside me on the couch, Jason's elderly neighbor

is going on about his problem with chipmunks in his cellar. "They're cute until they chew through your wires," he says.

Mrs. Morehouse answers the doorbell. "Thank you for inviting us." I hear Mom's voice. "David's been looking forward to this all afternoon."

"Now I don't think about cute," the man next to me says. "I think about that electrician's bill."

Before I can greet Mom and David, David rushes past me. "Cake?"

I keep David in my line of sight as he sits at the kitchen table — especially as Mrs. Morehouse shows Mom something out the window.

"How lovely," Mom says. "Are they hard to grow? My husband is the gardener in our family."

I stand up. "Nice to meet you," I say to the chipmunk man as I watch David slide his hand toward the platter of leftover cake. "And, um, good luck."

"Darn little pests." He turns to the woman on his other side. "If you've got one, you've got a whole bunch."

I hurry to the kitchen and drop my plate of cake in

front of David. “Use a fork,” I whisper, pressing mine into his hand. “Not your fingers.”

Around me a woman rinses cups in the sink, and Matt scrapes crumbs from his plate into the trash. A teenaged girl with braids brings a baby in, his mouth ringed brown with frosting. “Can I have some extra napkins?” she asks.

Jason comes up beside me. Sorry. Neighbor. Talk. All the time.

“No problem. My old neighbor, Mrs. Bowman, used to talk a lot, too.”

Sorry. Catherine. New. Neighbor. Friend. Can’t. Come. My birthday party.

“I’m sure Kristi would’ve had fun.” I throw David a strict look as he picks a bite of cake off his plate with his fingers. “But the community center dance is tonight, and she had to help decorate.”

Do you want to come? Dance.

“No. She’s going with Ryan. I’m sure he doesn’t want me hanging around with them, any more than I want to be with him.”

David licks frosting off the side of his hand. I

pass him a napkin, but he wipes his mouth with it instead.

I mean. Do you want to come? Dance. Me.

I look up from Jason's book. He's watching my face, his eyes serious.

"I can't."

Why?

I stare at the word card with its big question mark.

Are? You. Embarrassed. About. Me.

"Of course not!" I hear Jason pound his cards, but I can't look. I brush crumbs off David's shirt into my cupped hand. "I'm just a horrible dancer. Terrible. In fact, I'm so bad I even have a rule against it. No dancing unless I'm alone in my room or it's pitch-black dark."

Jason makes a loud, rumbling sound. RULE. Stupid. Excuse.

My breath catches. Everyone in the kitchen has stopped to look at us, except David, who pushes back his chair.

"My rules aren't stupid," I say quietly, "or excuses."

Yes. Excuse. I. Just. Like. Music. He scowls. And.

YOU. Ramming the joystick forward, Jason whirrs out of the kitchen, past David opening a cupboard door.

"More cake?" David asks as I pry his fingers off the door handle.

"We're all done." Holding his arm, I pull him behind me. "Excuse me," I say, passing people. "Sorry, gotta go."

"Catherine?" Mom asks. "Is something wrong?"

I push open the door. Tears spill down my cheeks as I run with David down the ramp.

The party's over.

Some people think they know who you are, when really they don't.

My head against the car window, I cross my legs and arms, folding the ache inside. Beside me, David holds his hands over his ears.

"Did David do something to upset you?" Mom asks.

Unbelievable! I look up to the rearview mirror. "You were supposed to watch him! You promised!"

"I could see him," she says. "He wasn't doing any harm."

"He was opening doors!"

"So what? He opened one door." Her eyes flash to mine in the mirror. "For goodness' sakes, Jason's family understands."

"Understands what? That we're as different as they are? Is that supposed to make it okay?"

"Shh," Mom says, her eyes moving to David.

I look at him, wishing he'd take his hands off his ears and say, "It's going to be all right, Catherine. Don't worry," or "I'll try harder next time," or even "I'm sorry."

But he only sits, rocking gently, a faraway smile on his face.

"Do you want me to call Mrs. Morehouse and apologize?" Mom asks.

"It's too late." I turn to stare unfocused out the window, the side of the road becoming a sand-colored smear. "Jason asked me to the community center dance. When I said no, he asked if I was embarrassed about him."

"Are you?" Mom asks.

"No . . . well . . . the rest of the world isn't like the clinic. Other places, people stare. Or they hurry away, and I know what they're thinking. 'Oh, isn't that too bad,' or 'What's wrong with that kid?' or 'Whew, I'm glad that's not me.' I get so sick of it."

"Just because other people think something, that doesn't make it true."

Maybe there's some truth in that, but it's unsatisfying, bitter-tasting truth. I glance at David. "It doesn't make it easy, either."

"No, it doesn't make it easy."

David stops rocking and gives me a fleeting look. "I'm sorry, Frog."

For once, Mom doesn't correct him.

At home Mom says she has to drop paperwork off at a few clients' houses. "You can both come or you can babysit David."

"I'll babysit." I've had enough of David at other people's houses for one day. I dump a puzzle on the living room floor, glad for the simple right and wrong of a single, perfect fit.

"Where's the sky, Frog?" David asks, beside me.

I hunt for sky-blue and cloud-white pieces. First, the top-left corner, then another straight-edged piece of blue. I hold up a cloud. "I think this is next."

David's hand shoots out, grabs the piece from my fingers, and snaps it in place.

Piece by piece, the sky appears, a put-together line

of blue and white. Reaching the top-right corner, David hunts for the second row of pieces, sharp-pointed roofs and the tops of trees.

I leave him leaning over the puzzle, his hair falling forward as he picks up pieces and discards them, one after one.

In my room I open my sketchbook to the page with 'guilty,' 'complicated,' 'hidden,' and 'weak.'

Out the window, Kristi's driveway is empty, and I don't even care. I miss Melissa. I miss how she goes swimming at the pond with me and isn't afraid. I miss how we build mazes and guinea-pig playgrounds on my floor for Cinnamon and Nutmeg. I miss being myself with my friend and not having to try so hard.

If she were home, I could tell Melissa everything about Jason and Kristi and she wouldn't laugh unless I did.

"Fix it?" David stands behind me. I didn't even hear him come in.

"Next time, don't forget to knock." I hold out my hand and feel a cassette dropped on my palm. But when I look, there are two long lines of tape hanging down, snapped.

David folds my fingers around his cassette. "You can fix it?"

"No."

He puts his hand over his ears. "Don't worry. You can fix it."

"You don't get it. I can't fix it!" I throw the cassette. It clangs, hitting the bottom of my trash can.

"Fix it!" David screams.

"When someone is upset, it's not a good time to bring up your own problems!" I scream back. "Why don't you understand? No toys in the fish tank! Chew with your mouth closed! Don't open or close doors at other people's houses!"

David drops to the floor and wraps his arms over his knees. "Trash goes in the garbage can," he says, between sobs. "That's the rule."

He's crying so hard, his whole body shakes. I get David's cassette from the trash, but it's too broken. "I can't fix it."

Tears fill my eyes. I walk over and kneel beside him. Circling his knees and shoulders with my arms, I lay my chin on David's hair.

"I'm sorry," I whisper. "I'm sorry, Toad."

Each phone ring sounds like a long breath in my ear. One ring-breath. *Please be home.* Beside me, David leans against my arm.

Two rings. *Please listen.*

Three. *Please —*

"Hello?"

"Hi. This is Catherine."

When Mrs. Morehouse doesn't say anything, for a split second I think about hanging up, but somehow I squeeze the words around the lump in my throat. "Can I talk to Jason?"

Mrs. Morehouse pauses. "Just a minute."

Waiting, my heart throbs: *please, please, please.*

"Catherine?" Mrs. Morehouse says. "He doesn't want to come to the phone."

"Would you tell him something for me? Would you

tell him I'm sorry, and I'd like to invite him to the dance tonight."

She sighs. "I don't know."

"I'll be there in an hour. Please tell him I really want him to come." I give her the details, even though she won't even promise to tell him.

Hanging up, I say to David, "Now we're calling Dad."

The pharmacy worker who answers the phone tells me Dad's busy, but I say it's an emergency.

"Catherine! What's wrong?" Dad asks.

"You need to come home," I say. "But on the way, you need to stop at the mall and buy a cassette of *Frog and Toad Together* by Arnold Lobel. It's very important. Are you writing this down?"

"Catherine, I have to —"

"We matter, too!" I snap. "You need to buy *Frog and Toad Together* by Arnold Lobel and a new cassette player and come home *now*."

"Of course you matter, just give me a few —"

I hang up.

After changing into my favorite jean skirt and black

tank top, I sit on the front porch with David, brushing my hair and watching the road.

Twenty-three cars later, Dad drives in the driveway.

"Come on, David." I take his hand. "I'm going to a dance."

Late doesn't mean not coming.

I hear music. The double doors to the town community center are propped wide open, a rectangle of yellow light spread on the sidewalk.

David jumps into the box of light. He waves his fingers in excitement, watching his shadow.

"Catherine, next time, you need to plan better," Dad says. "I can't leave work for something like this."

I watch David jumping, his shadow hands fluttering. "You take David to the video store every time he has OT."

"That's different."

"Different because it's *him*?"

Dad huffs, turning to me. "David needs —"

"I *know* what he needs! Believe me!" I push my way

past Dad, not even caring that I'm yelling. "Maybe he *does* need you more than me, but that doesn't mean I don't need anything at all!"

"Go inside?" David asks as I step on his shadow.

"Ask Dad. He's in charge." My throat is raw. Looking ahead to the community center, I've never felt so alone.

I hear footsteps coming up behind me. "Cath?"

"I have to matter, too," I say. "As much as work and your garden and even as much as David. I need you, too."

I feel his arm go around me, turning me to face his shoulder. "You matter," Dad says, holding me.

Even though strangers glance at us as they pass, I hold him tight. "Would you stay until I know if Jason's coming?"

"Sure."

My forehead pressed into the hollow of Dad's shoulder, his shirt smells sickly sweet, like cherry cough syrup from the pharmacy, but I don't care. "And can I borrow some money? I spent all mine on Jason's present."

Dad digs in his pocket with his free hand. "Here's extra so you can call me when you're ready to come home. I'll come as soon as you call."

"Go inside?" David asks.

I nod. "I'm ready."

Inside the doors a woman looks up from the admission table. The poster I made is taped on the wall behind her. "Welcome," she says, opening her cash box. "Are you here for the dance?"

"My daughter is. My son and I are only here until her friend comes." Dad pays for all of us, but David doesn't want his hand stamped.

"Watch. It doesn't hurt." I hold my hand out and the lady says, "Would you like a flower or a frog or a dragonfly?"

"A frog, please."

She presses the stamp onto the back of my hand and I show David. "Look, it's Frog."

David holds his hand out to me, and I turn it over so she can stamp the back.

"Something smells good," Dad says.

"We have a bake sale going on, and there's popcorn

and soda." The woman points down the hall toward tables piled with brownies and cookies. "Everything is fifty cents or a dollar, but you can't bring food or drinks in the gym."

"It's the rule," David says.

Ahead there's a scatter of flyers on the bulletin board, and the doorway to the gym is surrounded with colored streamers and twinkly white Christmas lights.

Dad stops to talk to someone at a long table selling T-shirts with the community center logo on them, and I hear snips of the conversation: "lots of kids," "lovely night," "the pharmacy is good."

Beside me David steps close to the lights, his fingers flickering at his sides, fast as moth wings.

"The lights are beautiful, aren't they?" I say. "Like hundreds of stars."

"Like stars," David says. "Make a wish, Frog."

I close my eyes and reach in my skirt pocket, fingering the money Dad gave me. From inside the gym, a song starts — a fast, wonderful, bursting-with-life song.

When I open my eyes, David's staring at me, inches from my face.

Most people say if you tell a wish it won't come true. But I don't think wishes work like that. I don't believe there's some bad-tempered wish-fairy with a clipboard, checking off whether or not you've told. *Oops! You told your wish. No new bike for you!* But it's a long shot I'll get my wish, so even if there is a fairy in charge of telling, it won't matter.

"I wish everyone had the same chances," I say. "Because it stinks a big one that they don't. What about you? What did you wish for?"

"Grape soda."

I can't help smiling. "You wished for *grape soda*?"

He doesn't answer, and I pull my hand from my pocket. Taking one of his fluttering hands, I wrap his fingers tightly around a dollar. "Wish granted, Toad."

He takes off running, and Dad runs after him.

I close my eyes and make a new wish.

I wish the refreshment stand has grape soda.

A real conversation takes two people.

Alone on the bleachers I run my hands over my knees to wipe the sweat away. In the half-lit gym, the white stripes on the floor and the basketball backboards almost glow. My fingers long for a fat paintbrush to stroke color across the white backboards: bloodred, electric blue, tangerine — blistering colors.

But I have nothing to hold and nothing to do but wait.

I've checked all along the sides of the gym, across the dance floor, out in the hallway, even past the little offices holding sports equipment. The lit clock above the EXIT sign barely moves, and I make deals with myself. He'll come when the minute hand is on the four.

The music blares. I can't hear my feet tap, but

someone must've spilled a drink because my sandals catch on something sticky. Worry twines in my chest, and I keep unsticking my feet, in case I need to run out to find Dad and tell him I want to go home, now. I last saw him and David drinking grape sodas on the stairs.

Jason'll come when the minute hand is on the six.

Watching kids dancing, I flicker my fingers on my knees. Some of the dancers look goofy — one boy reminds me of David, his elbows bent sharply. But there are so many kids, it doesn't matter. The other dancers make room for him.

I see kids from school I recognize, but no Kristi or Ryan.

My fingers trace a cut in the wood of the bleacher beside me, over and over. I slide my fingers along the groove, feeling every bump.

Jason'll come when the minute hand is on the eleven.

It's hot inside the gym from all the kids, and I wish I could get a drink or step outside and breathe some cooler air, but I'm afraid I'll miss Jason. So I lean back, rest my elbows on the bleacher behind me, and look at the ceiling. I imagine the beams gone, the roof pulled away, only the endless night sky above me, full of stars.

The song ends, and kids fill in the bleachers around me. Some kids turn back to the dance floor as another song begins. It hurts how life goes on, unknowing. All these kids walking by, heading to the dance floor or toward the hallway.

Not even seeing me.

I watch a girl move toward the door. In the bright light from the hallway, she darkens to a shadow, passing the outline of a wheelchair in the doorway.

"Sorry! Excuse me!" I step around knees and feet, trying not to push but wanting to shove past everyone. "I have to get over there."

As I come closer, Jason looks at me, eyes narrowing. Mrs. Morehouse stands at his side.

"I'm glad you're here," I say. "I really wanted to talk to you."

"I'll be in the hall where it's quieter," Mrs. Morehouse says. "Come get me if you need me."

"Excuse me," I call over and over to kids' backs, making room for us to move down the quiet hallway outside the community center offices. Through the windows, I see the dark outline of grape clusters of basketballs, stacks of pointed traffic cones, and a rack of hockey sticks.

Standing next to Jason, I don't know what to say to get started. "It's a nice night out."

Jason turns his wheelchair to leave.

"Wait!" I reach into my skirt pocket and pull out my first word. Complicated.

Jason lifts his eyebrows.

I kneel to be at his eye level. "I see how kids stare at David and it hurts me, because I know what they're thinking. Or even worse, they *don't* look at him, just around him, like he's invisible. It makes me mad, because it's mean and it makes me invisible, too."

Jason watches my face, but his hand moves to give me room to reach the last empty pockets of his communication book.

Hidden. "I didn't tell Kristi everything about you. I didn't tell her about your wheelchair or your communication book. I didn't know how she'd react. I should've because you're my friend, but it got harder and harder." I drop my gaze to the tiled floor. "No, that's an excuse, too. The real truth is I was scared what she might think of *me*, not you."

When I look up, Jason is staring toward the dark windows of the community center offices.

"You're a good friend," I say, "and I've been —"

Weak.

"Catherine?"

I knew this moment was coming, but I still feel caught red-handed. Kristi hurries up the hall, wearing white jeans and a bright pink shirt. "I thought you couldn't come! I'm so happy you changed your mind."

Beside her, Ryan puts his hand on her arm.

I stand up. "Jason, this is Ryan and my next-door neighbor, Kristi."

Her smile slips. "Hi."

"Kristi, this is Jason."

She glances from Ryan to me to Jason. "Uh, happy birthday."

Thank you.

Kristi looks at me, one eyebrow raised.

"Jason can't talk so he uses these cards, and I've been making words for him." I smile at Jason. "He's my very good —" I tap, Friend.

She looks where I'm pointing, to the card of a girl's hand waving.

Jason taps, Catherine. Talk. About. You. All the time.

"Really?" Kristi makes a *hmm* sound. "She could've told me more about you."

Ryan pulls Kristi's arm. "Come on, Kris."

"I'm sorry," I say. "I should've told you the truth."

"Yeah," she says flatly, not looking at me. "You should've. I'll see you around."

As they walk away, I open my hand to show Jason my last card. "I have one more."

He shakes his head. Don't. Want. It.

I fold Guilty. until it's so small it won't fold again.

Jason starts his wheelchair down the hall.

"Wait," I say, rushing to catch up. "Where are you going?"

Dance. Do you want to come?

"But I don't —"

Break. Dance. RULE. Jason tips his head down, looking under his eyebrows at me, like he's expecting me to blast off on a wild, chatty detour. And a detour sits on my tongue like an airplane waiting on the run-way. *All systems go, cleared for takeoff.*

"All right." I follow him down the hallway and out across the dark gym floor to the very center where there's a clearing in the kids.

Next to me a girl lifts her arms above her head. One by one the other dancers join her, palms reaching upward, swaying back and forth.

Jason joins them, palms open. Standing there, in the middle of the floor, in front of everyone, I lift my hands and reach for the ceiling, the sky, the stars.

And I dance.

If you need to borrow words,

Arnold Lobel wrote some good ones.

Before I climb into bed, I circle the date on my calendar when Melissa will be home. I have so much to tell her, not the least of which is I danced with a boy who isn't even related to me, and I liked it.

And on Tuesday, I'm not bringing my backpack to the clinic, only me. If Jason needs a word I'll make it, but I'll wait for him to ask.

I lift my shade and imagine a beam flashing from Kristi's dark window, counting dashes and dots.

A-r-e y-o-u t-h-e-r-e?

But there is no light. Her window stays dark, only the streetlamps and the stars shine, white brightness.

The tiniest knock comes, and my door creaks open.

David stands framed in the light from the living room. "No toys in the fish tank."

I slide my slippers on and follow.

In the aquarium a toy wizard stands on the gravel, his wand raised, mid-spell. Standing beside the castle, he's so big only his pointy shoe would fit through the tiny castle door.

Oops! Wrong spell!

And instead of a fierce dragon to slay, a huge, curious goldfish mouths the end of the wizard's hat.

I can't help but laugh.

"'"What are you laughing at, Frog?"'" David asks, worried lines cutting his forehead.

I touch the tiny frog stamp on his hand and show him mine. "'"I am laughing at you, Toad," said Frog, "because you *do* look funny in your bathing suit."'"

David smiles. "'"Of course I do," said Toad. Then he picked up his clothes and went home.'"

"The end."

Tomorrow I'm going to tell Mom she has a point about David needing his own words, but other things matter, too. Like sharing something small and special, just my brother and me.

Kneeling beside David, our arms touching, our faces reflect side by side, in the glass.

I let that be enough.

AFTER WORDS™

CYNTHIA LORD'S

Rules

CONTENTS

After Words™ guide by Cassandra Pelham

About the Author

Cynthia Lord grew up next to a lake in rural New Hampshire. As a child, she loved to read and create stories. The earliest writing she remembers doing was a goofy song called "Ding Dong the Cherries Sing," which she wrote at the age of four with her sister and forced everyone to listen to over and over. As Cynthia grew up, she wrote poems, newspaper articles, and stories.

As an adult, when Cynthia sat down to write her first children's book, she knew it would be a middle-grade novel. As she recalls, "I remember being ten years old, lying on our pier, listening to the seagulls calling, and daydreaming about Borrowers and chocolate factories and secret gardens."

A former teacher and bookseller, Cynthia still enjoys nature and reading a good book. And shc hears plenty of seagulls at her home near the ocean in Maine, where she lives with her husband and two children. She says, "Though I have children of my own now, when I write it's always for that daydreaming girl I used to be."

Rules, a Newbery Honor winner and *New York Times* bestseller, is Cynthia's first novel. Visit her on the Web at www.cynthialord.com.

Q&A with Cynthia Lord

Q: *Where did the idea for* Rules *come from?*

A: I have two children, a daughter and a son, and my son has autism. One day when my daughter was about ten years old, she asked me, "Mom, how come I never see families like mine in books and on TV?" I didn't know how to answer her, so I went looking for children's books that included characters with severe special needs. I did find some, but most of the books I read seemed very sad to me. Sadness is part of living with someone with a severe disability, but it's only one part. It can also be funny, inspiring, heartwarming, disappointing, frustrating—everything that it is to love *anyone* and to live in any family.

Q: *How much did you draw on your own family for this book? Are your kids anything like Catherine and David?*

A: The biggest elements in *Rules* are from my imagination. The characters are not my own family and the story itself isn't true. Some of the small details in the book are real, though. My son used to repeat lines from books, and he loved Arnold Lobel's stories. He also liked to drop things in our fish tank, which frustrated me. Then one day I realized I was the only person who minded (the fish loved having company!). It started me thinking about all those social "rules" we follow, sometimes without even knowing why. Catherine is more like me than my daughter. My daughter is an artist, though. So she was a big help when I was writing the scenes where Catherine is drawing.

Q: *What were you like as a child?*

A: I grew up in a house beside a lake in a small town in New Hampshire. As a child, I liked to go exploring on my bike. I also loved to play my clarinet in the school band (though I didn't always like to practice!), imagine stories, teach my dog new tricks, go swimming with my friends, and read.

Q: *What is your writing process like? Do you have a special place or time of day?*

A: My writing day starts before dawn. I usually get up around four in the morning. That routine started when my children were small, because it was the one time I could depend on. Now I get up early, just because I love that time of day. It's quiet and peaceful and I like to see the sun come up. I live in Maine near the coast, so in the summer, I open the window beside my desk, and I can smell the ocean. My dog gets up with me, and then he goes to sleep near my feet while I write. I also go to my local library to work sometimes in the afternoons.

Q: *What was your favorite part of writing* Rules?

A: I loved so many parts, but writing the dialogue between the guinea pigs was especially fun.

Q: *How did Jason's character come to you?*

A: My own son has had years of occupational and speech therapy appointments. One day, when I was waiting for him to finish his session, a boy and his mother came into the clinic waiting room. The boy used a wheelchair and a communication book, like Jason does. He and his mom were having an argument, and two things really struck me. First, I was surprised that someone *could* have an argument using a communication book. Second, I realized he could only use words that someone else had given him. I wondered if there were words he wished he had. That boy isn't Jason (because I don't know that boy), but that's where his character began for me.

Q: *What do you do when you're not writing?*
A: I like to read, watch movies and TV, and walk beside the ocean. I spend a lot of time traveling and answering mail from readers, which is always fun. I also love to be home with my family and my dog.

Q: *One of Catherine's rules for David is "Not everything worth keeping has to be useful." What is your favorite possession?*
A: I have many special possessions, but one of my favorites is my Newbery Honor award. When I look at it, I know that dreams can come true.

Q: *Catherine has two guinea pigs, Nutmeg and Cinnamon, and then of course there are the family fish. Are there any pets at your house?*

A: I love animals, so we've had so many pets over the years. We've had hamsters, mice, guinea pigs, gerbils, fish, frogs, and dogs at our house. At the moment, we only have one dog. His name is Milo, and he's half Pomeranian and half Maltese. He looks like a baby polar bear, because he's all white, except for his black eyes and nose.

Q: *I hear you have a pretty extensive rubber duck collection. How and when did that start?*

A: I love *Rules'* cover. The first time I saw it, I thought it looked appealing and fun, but there was one problem. There was no rubber duck in my story. I thought to myself, "Kids will expect a duck in this book," and so I traded one of the toys that David drops in the fish tank for a rubber duck right before *Rules* was published. Now, people give me ducks! I have duck pen holders, duck wall hangings, duck ornaments, duck toys, and lots of rubber ducks. I've discovered them on my signing table at events, floating in punch bowls, in my Christmas stocking, etc. It's great fun!

A few ducks from Cynthia's collection

Q: *What do you hope readers will take away from* Rules?

A: First, I hope they will simply enjoy the story. But beyond that, I also hope that meeting David and Jason in *Rules* will help readers to have less fear and more understanding toward the people with disabilities in their own communities and schools.

A New Set of Rules

Catherine creates rules for her younger brother David to help him understand how other people behave and how the world works. Have you ever wanted to make up a list of rules for a member of your own family? Well, now you can! Take a look at the examples below that you may want to use, and feel free to add your own!

- Don't follow me everywhere I go (unless we're playing Follow the Leader).
- Knock first!
- If you want to play with one of my toys, please put it back when you're done.
- Take my side when someone is teasing me.
- Never say mean things like, "The dog likes me better!"
- Don't borrow my clothes without asking, and be extra careful not to spill anything on them!
- No spying or snooping on me when I'm with my friends.
- Sometimes I get to choose what we'll do, and sometimes you get to decide.
- Say yes (sometimes, at least!) when I ask you to play with me.
- Don't hog the computer or the phone or the TV.
- When I'm upset, ask me, "Why?" Then listen.

Inside Catherine's Sketchbook

Catherine never goes anywhere without her sketchbook. Learn how to draw a guinea pig by following the steps below!

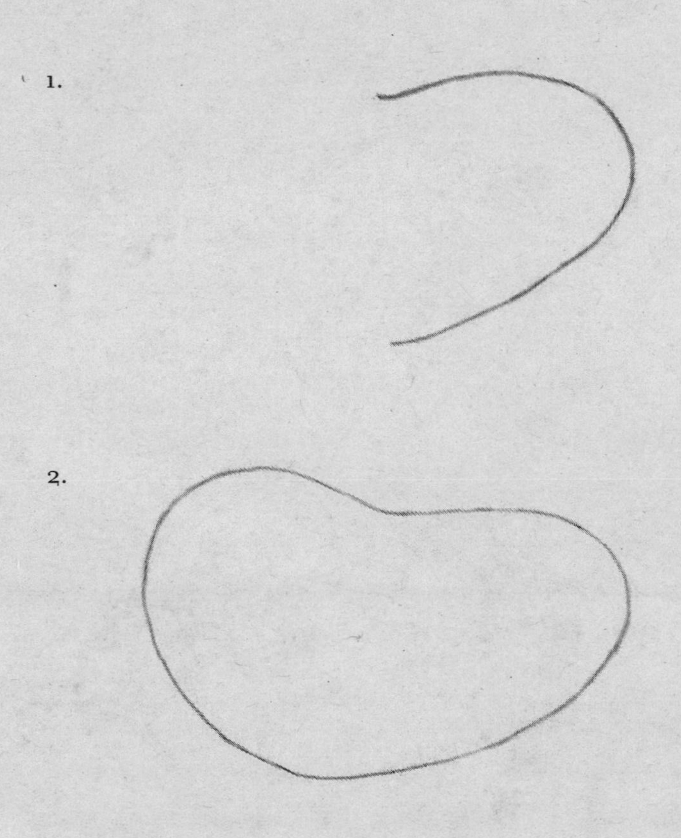

3.
4.
5.

Dots and Dashes: Messages in Morse Code

Morse code, named after Samuel F. B. Morse, is a way of sending messages with symbols and sounds. Dots (which make the sound "dit") and dashes (which make the sound "dah") make up the Morse code alphabet. In *Rules*, Catherine hopes for a next-door friend who would find it fun to send flashlight messages in Morse code between their windows at night. Using the Morse code alphabet pictured below as a guide, have fun decoding these words and phrases.

The Morse Code Alphabet

A	.–	**N**	–.
B	–...	**O**	–––
C	–.–.	**P**	.––.
D	–..	**Q**	––.–
E	.	**R**	.–.
F	..–.	**S**	...
G	––.	**T**	–
H	....	**U**	..–
I	..	**V**	...–
J	.–––	**W**	.––
K	–.–	**X**	–..–
L	.–..	**Y**	–.––
M	––	**Z**	––..

1. —.—. .— — .... . .—. .. —. .

2. —.. .— ...— .. —..

3. .——— .— ... ——— —.

4. —.— .—. .. ... — ..

5. —. ..— — —— . ——. .— —. —..
—.—. .. —. —. .— —— ——— —.

6. ..—. .—. ——— ——. .— —. —..
— ——— .— —..

7. —. ——— — ——— —.—— ... .. —.
— ....—. .. .. — .— —. —.—

8. ... — .. —. —.— ... .— —... .. ——.
——— —. .!

9. —.. .. —.. —.—— ——— ..—
. —. .——— ——— —.—— — ....
—... ——— ——— —.—?

10. — .... .— —. —.— —.—— ——— ..—
..—. ——— .—. .—. . .— —.. .. —. ——.!

Answers:

1. Catherine 2. David 3. Jason 4. Kristi 5. Nutmeg and Cinnamon
6. Frog and Toad 7. No toys in the fish tank! 8. Stinks a big one!
9. Did you enjoy this book? 10. Thank you for reading!

Further Reading

If you liked *Rules*, here are some other books you might enjoy!

Al Capone Does My Shirts by Gennifer Choldenko
Set on Alcatraz Island in 1935, this poignant novel is told from the viewpoint of Moose, a boy both frustrated by and fiercely committed to his sister with autism.

A Corner of the Universe by Ann M. Martin
Twelve-year-old Hattie develops a sensitive friendship with her Uncle Adam, a man challenged by schizophrenia and autism, during the summer he comes to live at her family's boarding house.

Me and Rupert Goody by Barbara O'Connor
Eleven-year-old Jennalee's world is turned upside down when a man with developmental delays arrives in her town in the Smoky Mountains, claiming to be the son of the grocer Jennalee looks up to as her best friend.

My Thirteenth Winter: A Memoir by Samantha Abeel
Samantha describes in painstaking detail her life before and after being diagnosed with dyscalculia, a math-related learning disability.

The Summer of the Swans by Betsy Byars
Fourteen-year-old Sara Godfrey and her developmentally delayed brother Charlie love to watch the swans on a local lake, until Charlie disappears one day and Sarah must reach past herself to find him.

Tru Confessions by Janet Tashjian
Told through diary entries, twelve-year-old Tru creates a film documentary highlighting the life of her developmentally delayed twin brother.

Views from Our Shoes: Growing Up with a Brother or Sister with Special Needs edited by Donald J. Meyer
This is a collection of honest, small essays written by siblings of children with a broad range of special needs.

Watch for

Cynthia Lord's second novel

Touch Blue,

coming soon!

On a tiny island off the coast of Maine, twelve-year-old Tess anxiously awaits the arrival of her new foster brother, Aaron. He'll be a good match, according to the caseworker. She'll welcome him and act like he's just another islander, according to her parents. But the moment Aaron steps from the ferry, Tess's excitement turns to worry: How can *this* boy be a match?

Through wholehearted, sparkling prose Newbery Honor author Cynthia Lord offers a gentle reminder that belonging doesn't always mean fitting in and that standing up for oneself sometimes means rocking the boat. *Touch Blue*, sure as certain, will touch your heart.